THE DARKEST EVENING

WILLIAM DURBIN

ORCHARD BOOKS

NEW YORK

AN IMPRINT OF

SCHOLASTIC INC.

ACKNOWLEDGMENTS

This book would not have been possible without the help of the following individuals who assisted in my research: Nick Baron, Ph.D., University of Manchester, England; Steve Harsin and Deb Fena, Ironworld Research Center; Michael Karni, Ph.D., Sampo Publishing; James Kurtti, Editor, *Finnish American Review*; Rik Laiho; Harry Lamppa and Betty Birnstihl, Virginia Area Historical Society; Heather Marstall, Wind River Bear Institute; Anita Middleton; Tom Morgan, College of St. Scholastica, Duluth, Minnesota; Daniel Necas, Immigration History Research Center, University of Minnesota; Annikki Ojala, Lehtimäki, Finland; Cindy Outhouse, Karelian bear dog expert, Likely, British Columbia; Mary Ann Paulin, Lake Superior Preview Center; Alexis Pogereltzin, Ph.D., University of Minnesota Duluth; Alpo Rissanen, Suomussalmi, Finland; Mark Rouleau, Palucci Planetarium; and the staffs of the Minnesota Historical Society, University of Minnesota Duluth Library, and the Hibbing and Virginia public libraries.

And special thanks to my editor, Amy Griffin, for her insight and patience; to my agent, Barbara Markowitz, who is both an advocate and a friend; to my wife, Barbara, my first and best critic; and to Jessica and Reid, who consistently make their father proud.

LIBRARY OF CONGRESS CATALOGING-IN-PUBLICATION DATA

Durbin, William, 1951 – The darkest evening / by William Durbin.

p. cm

Summary: In the 1930s, a young Finnish-American boy reluctantly moves with his family to Karelia, a Communist Finnish state founded in Russia, where his idealistic father soon realizes that his conception of a Communist utopia is flawed.

[Fic]—22   2003020255

ISBN 0-439-37307-7

[1. Finnish Americans — Russia (Federation) — Karelia — Juvenile fiction. 2. Finnish Americans — Russia (Federation) — Karelia — Fiction. 3. Emigration and immigration — Fiction. 4. Communism — Fiction. 5. Karelia (Russia) — Fiction. 6. Russia (Federation) — History — 20th century — Fiction.]

10 9 8 7 6 5 4 3 2 1

08 07 06 05 04

Printed in the U.S.A. 37

First American edition, November 2004

The text type was set in 12-pt Hoefler Text

Book design by David Caplan

To the memory of those
who lived this story,
and to Mayme Sevander,
who helped me see
Karelia through her eyes.

FOREWORD

IN THE EARLY 1930S, RUSSIAN RECRUITERS VISITED FINNISH-AMERICAN COMMUNITIES ALL ACROSS THE NORTHERN UNITED STATES AND CANADA AND CONVINCED SOME 6,000 NORTH AMERICAN FINNS TO MIGRATE TO THE PROVINCE OF KARELIA, RUSSIA. MOTIVATED BY POLITICAL IDEALISM, THE SPIRIT OF ADVENTURE, AND THE PROMISE OF FULL EMPLOYMENT AND FREE EDUCATION, THE FINNS WILLINGLY SOLD THEIR POSSESSIONS AND BOARDED SHIPS FOR RUSSIA. THIS NOVEL TELLS THE STORY OF ONE FAMILY WHO SET OUT ON THAT BOLD JOURNEY.

PART I
IN SEARCH OF
THE MIDNIGHT SUN
FEBRUARY 1934
THE MESABI IRON RANGE • VIRGINIA, MINNESOTA

BOOT STEPS IN THE NIGHT

They were coming for him. Under a winter moon the soldiers marched. Boot heels pounded out a perfect rhythm on the frozen street as they drew ever closer and ever louder. Jake saw black uniforms in rows of three. Shoulders back. Arms stiff. Faces lost in shadow. The marching grew louder and louder. Steam rose from fur-capped heads. They were coming for him. They were coming for him.

Suddenly a shout split the night. "It isn't fair!"

"Please, Arvid," a second voice pleaded. "Not so loud. The children are sleeping."

Jake opened his eyes and blinked in the cold blue moonlight. The marching was only Father pacing on the wooden

I

floor in the kitchen below his bedroom. "How do they expect the miners to live on one day of work per week?"

"Most families are grateful," Mother said. "Surely one shift is better than nothing at all."

"It's time people wake up to the fact that the mining companies are bleeding this town dry." Father's voice boomed through the floor.

Jake's older brother, Peter, who shared the creaky bed with him, groaned in his sleep and turned over. Father no longer worked in the iron ore mines, but his job at the Finntown Cooperative Store depended on the business of the miners.

"Quiet your voice, Arvid," Mother said. "The Depression has made things hard everywhere."

"But why does it always have to be hardest on the Finns?"

Mother started to say something, but she stopped.

Before Father could speak again, Jake covered his head with his pillow.

"Rise and shine, Hub." Peter tapped Jake's shoulder with the baseball glove that Jake always kept on the nightstand beside the bed. As a joke Peter called Jake "Hub," the nickname of his favorite player, Carl Hubbell.

"Is it morning already?" Jake yawned.

"I'm afraid so. Father's preaching must have kept you up."

"I thought you slept through it all." Jake rubbed his eyes with the back of his knuckles.

"I heard my share," Peter said as he picked up his schoolbooks. Though Peter was four years older and a half foot taller, he and Jake could have been twins. Both boys were broad-shouldered and blue-eyed, with white-blond hair. But beyond their looks, they were totally different. While Jake liked to play sports and tinker with machines, Peter preferred mathematics and music.

"Father's so bullheaded, he's like a locomotive with the throttle stuck wide open," Jake said.

"That locomotive is going to be headed straight for you if you don't get up soon." Peter laughed as he headed downstairs.

By the time Jake had dressed and washed his face, Peter and his little sister, Maija, were finishing their breakfast. Mother stood at the cookstove, humming softly to herself, and Father was reading his newspaper. "I called you twice, Jaakko," Mother said, speaking Finnish as she always did and setting a bowl of oatmeal in front of him.

"I'm sorry," Jake said. The kitchen smelled of hot coffee and sweetbread dough.

"Your father had to shovel the coal for the furnace." Mother stepped back from the stove and wiped her hands on her apron. "That's the second time this week you've forgotten."

"I had trouble sleeping," Jake said. By the redness of Mother's eyes, Jake could tell that she hadn't slept well either.

"Lazybones," Maija said, holding her lips tight.

"Miss Perfect," Jake said. His eight-year-old sister always pretended that she could do no wrong. Maija had blond hair like Father and the boys, but her face was dark complected and round like Mother's.

"There'll be no quarreling in my kitchen," Mother said.

"I'm sure Hub won't forget the furnace again, will you?" Peter winked at his brother as he got up from the table.

"I'll try not to," Jake said.

"See you tonight." Peter stepped onto the back porch and put on his coat.

"Keep up those straight A's," Father said.

"Good-bye, dear," Mother called.

Though Jake was only an average student, Peter had been nicknamed "the Genius" since he started playing the clarinet in fourth grade. He was so smart in science that he was taking chemistry this year as a tenth grader. But no matter how high his marks were, Peter stayed humble.

"You'd better get moving, too, little lady." Mother handed Maija her lunch box and steered her toward the back door.

As Jake took a spoonful of oatmeal, Father looked up from his copy of the *Työmies,* a socialist workers' newspaper. "It's time you learned to get yourself out of bed, young man." Father had a sharp-chinned face with a bushy mustache, and he was stoop shouldered from the many years he'd worked underground. "When I was your age, I did my chores without complaining. Then I put in a ten-hour shift, running drills to the miners in the Calumet and Hecla Copper Mine."

Father took a sip of his steaming black coffee, but instead of going back to his paper as Jake expected, he asked, "Don't you have anything to say for yourself?" Since Father usually lectured him without pausing for a reply, Jake didn't know what to say.

"Well?" Father's intense blue eyes flickered.

Jake swallowed a lump of oatmeal. "I'll try not to sleep late no more."

"Anymore," Father corrected him. Father always spoke

English with the children, and he made sure they used proper grammar. It seemed normal for Jake to speak two languages in his home. But when Jake's best friend, Joe Santelli, visited, Joe got confused. "My mom talks Italian to my grandma," Joe said, "but I can't see how you folks can understand each other when you switch from Finn to English in the middle of a sentence."

"Jaakko's English is better than your Finnish, Arvid," Mother teased, humming to herself as she finished mixing her dough in the big stone bowl. Barely five feet tall, Mother had strong hands and forearms from a lifetime of chopping wood, milking cows, and kneading bread.

Father chuckled. "You reindeer people don't even speak proper Finn, if you ask me."

"What would a pale Swede Finn like you know about proper Finnish?" Mother smiled. She was proud of her dark hair and brown eyes that came from her Laplander heritage. Mother's grandfather Lämsä was one of the reindeer people who had lived by following his herds all the way from Kuusamo, a small church village in northeastern Finland, to the arctic circle.

"At least I didn't grow up east of nowhere like your wandering Lämsä clan."

"I'd better get to school," Jake said, glad that Mother's teasing had distracted Father. Jake excused himself from the table and carried his oatmeal bowl to the sink.

"Study hard, dear," Mother said, brushing Jake's hair to one side. "Remind me to give you a haircut soon."

Jake stepped onto the porch and slipped on his hand-me-down wool coat. He grabbed his scarf from a hook, opened the door, and jumped off the back steps.

"Be careful, Jaakko. . . ." Mother's voice faded as he ran up the alley. The stinging cold on Jake's cheeks and the muffled sound of his heels hitting the packed snow told him that the temperature was twenty or thirty below.

Jake jogged down Third Street and turned up Second Avenue with his scarf trailing behind him. The stars were still bright above Finntown, but coal smoke hung low over the rooftops, leaving a sulfur taste in the back of Jake's throat.

"Hey, Jake." It was Joe, trotting out of the alley behind the Finnish Lutheran Church.

"Morning. You ready for your math test?"

"You know me and math," Joe said as they passed the Jukola boarding house. "I still haven't recovered from Miss Simmon's multiplication drills."

"We'd better hurry," Jake said, looking up the block at the students who were filing through the doors of the Lincoln School. The students were lining up at the nurse's office for their daily dose of cod-liver oil, a slimy medicine that gave them their vitamins. They'd all brought spoons from home last fall and written their names on a piece of adhesive tape that they'd stuck to the handles. By now the smeared names made it impossible for the students to tell whose spoon they were using, but the nurse said, "Move along now," as she poured out the thick oil and watched until everyone swallowed it. After a quick rinse under the drinking fountain, the spoons were tossed into her desk drawer, only to be pulled out again the next morning.

"Are you coming to the hockey rink tonight?" Joe asked as they turned up the school sidewalk.

Jake, who was still trying to decide whether the stink of the cod-liver oil or its fishy aftertaste was worse, grinned. "What else is there to do until baseball season starts?"

A TRIP TO THE OPERA

It was still so cold after school that Jake's eyelashes iced up on his short walk home. He pressed the back of his hands to his eyes as he walked into the kitchen. "You're frozen, Jaakko," Mother said. "You should wrap your scarf over your face."

"Is it okay if I play hockey after supper?" Jake asked, peering into the soup pot. The kitchen smelled of freshly baked bread and boiled potatoes.

"Your father wants us to go to a meeting this evening."

"Not again!" Jake moaned. "We've been listening to those Russian recruiters for years. You're not going to let Father move us to Karelia, are you?"

"I didn't come all the way from Finland to pack up again."

"And you'd be turning your back on the good luck pearl that bought you passage to America," Jake said.

"You never forget a story, do you?" Mother smiled. She'd often told the children about the day she found a huge freshwater pearl when she was swimming back in her village. The sale of the pearl allowed her to buy a steamship ticket and join her older sister in Michigan.

"So if we aren't moving, why waste our time going to those meetings?" Jake asked.

"It's only polite to listen, dear. Some of the brightest minds in America and Finland have dedicated themselves to creating a new Finnish state in Russia."

"What's wrong with Minnesota?"

"Why must you ask so many questions?" Mother said. "I swear you're cut from the same stubborn cloth as your father."

"I'm not like him," Jake said. "All he does is talk about the evil of the mining companies."

"If you'd lost your little sister, you'd feel the same way."

"I suppose," Jake said. Though Jake got tired of Father's constant complaining about the mine owners, he could understand his distrust. Father had grown up in Calumet,

Michigan, a town where the mining companies were all powerful. During a copper miners' strike on Christmas Eve in 1913, Father had taken his six-year-old sister, Liisa, to a children's party at the Italian Hall. A voice shouted, "Fire," and everyone ran down a narrow stairwell to escape. Liisa fell, but just as Father bent down to pick her up, he was slammed against the wall and knocked unconscious. When he woke up in the hospital, he learned that the fire had been a false alarm — most blamed it on a strikebreaker. Seventy-three people, including thirty-five children, died from being crushed and suffocated, among them little Liisa.

When they sat down to supper, Jake tried one last time to avoid the meeting. "Can I go over to the rink later?" he asked.

"Your mind is more important than chasing a hockey puck," Father said.

"I'm tired of hearing about those Marx and Engels fellows."

"Jaakko!" Mother said.

Jake knew better than to argue with his father, but he couldn't help it sometimes.

"That's all right, Annikki," Father said. "I encourage

my children to speak their minds. We're going as a family, Jake. You don't hear your brother or sister complaining, do you?"

Peter winked at Jake and grinned. Jake sighed. He knew that Peter found the meetings as boring as he did, but his brother was too polite to say anything. And Maija would do anything for Father's approval. She always took his side in arguments, and she sometimes even pretended to read Father's copy of *Das Kapital*.

Jake thought Father's socialist books and newspapers were dull. He would much rather be playing outside than sitting with a dusty book. When Jake did read, he chose adventure stories like *The Deerslayer* and *The Last of the Mohicans*, which Father called "trash."

"More soup, Arvid?" Mother asked, offering a ladleful of her fish-and-potato specialty.

Father shook his head and turned to Jake. "It's too bad you aren't excited about politics like Maija or music like Peter. You're a good boy, Jake, if you only had more drive."

"I'd rather do stuff than talk about ideas."

"Ideas replenish the soul," Father said.

The truth was Jake admired his mother's attitude toward life. Instead of railing against evil, she made the best of each day.

The Russian recruiter was lecturing at the Socialist Opera, a large hall next door to the Co-op Store. It was only four blocks from home, but Father insisted on leaving for the meeting a half hour early.

Father's janitor's job at the Co-op Store was another reason he wanted to leave the Iron Range. It was hard for Father to do menial labor, knowing he could be making three times the wages in the mines if he hadn't been blacklisted for joining the IWW union.

Jake dreaded another boring speech, but once he got inside the hall, he enjoyed studying the fancy murals and the globed chandelier. The speaker, Walter Harju, began like the other recruiters: "Look around you, and what do you see? Good Finnish men out of work. Women struggling to put bread on their tables. Every way you turn is proof that capitalism has failed."

Harju glanced from left to right. "Why should strong men like you labor in the darkness of the mines while John D. Rockefeller eats off gold plates? Instead of sweating to make the rich man richer, wouldn't you rather strive for the collective good of all?" Jake twisted in his seat. If the man hurried, Jake might be able to join the hockey game. "Even as I stand before you, Finnish men and women are gathering in Karelia, Russia, to build a workers' paradise where there is opportunity for all."

Jake couldn't deny the truth of what Harju said about rich folks getting all the money, but Jake believed in the liberty and freedom of American democracy. No matter how tough things got, he would never want to trade his life in the United States for an unknown future in a foreign land.

When the speaker warned that resettlement was only for men who were ready for the "ultimate test," Father sat up straighter.

Just when Jake thought the recruiter was done, he mentioned the wonderful education system in Russia. This was new to Jake. "Each and every student with talent can go to college free in the Soviet Union," he said. "It's not a closed system like in the U.S., where rich folks buy their sons and daughters degrees." Mother suddenly sat up as tall as Father. She listened as the man told how the students in Russia studied music and art and learned about Finnish culture. When he mentioned a city called Petrozavodsk, which had a symphony orchestra that immigrants could join, Mother whispered something to Father.

As soon as the speech was over, Mother and Father went

to the front of the auditorium and introduced themselves. Maija poked Jake's arm. "Can we go home now?"

"Just wait," Jake said, studying his parents' faces. He was hoping that Mother would shake her head as she had with the other recruiters, but this time she kept listening. Jake kept his hopes up until Mother pointed to Peter, and the recruiter smiled.

"Did you see that?" Jake asked.

Peter nodded. "Sorry, Hub. Just remember this wasn't my idea."

"What's taking so long?" Maija whined.

"They'll be done in a minute," Jake said. He turned to Peter. "I knew it was a mistake coming here tonight."

"By the look on Mother's face," Peter said, "I'll wager that we'll be ordering our passports very soon."

"What's a passport?" Maija asked.

"It's a ticket to the end of the world," Jake said.

A CHANGE OF SEASON

Jake soon forgot about the meeting with the recruiter and lost himself in a winter of hockey games and cross-country skiing. By late March, the snowbanks in the parking lot of the school had melted enough for Jake and Joe to play catch. One Saturday afternoon after a fun session of practicing their grounders by bouncing a rubber ball off the brick wall, Jake came home to find Father standing beside the kitchen table. "Look!" Father grinned, waving a letter. "Karelian Technical Aid has approved our application!"

"So soon?" Mother frowned.

"The Party must need our talents," Father said.

"Does that mean we're moving to Russia?" Maija tugged at Father's jacket. "Will we get to ride on a big ship?"

"We'd at least have to finish the school year first," Jake interrupted.

"There will be better schools in Russia," Father said. "And the sooner we get there, the sooner we can help."

"But Joe and I are going to try out for the baseball team."

"How can you worry about a silly game when we have a chance to build a new world?"

"Baseball's not silly." Jake spoke without thinking. "It's going off to Russia that's silly."

"Jaakko," Mother said. "Show respect."

"How can I show respect when my whole life is being ruined? You're asking me to give up everything I've ever known for — for a rotten country that's halfway around the world." Jake stopped. Father's unflinching eyes told him that his mind was made up. "What's the use?" Jake shook his head and walked downstairs. He spent the next hour throwing his rubber ball against the basement wall and catching the one-hoppers that caromed off the stones. *Why me?* he thought each time the ball smacked into his glove. *Why me?*

．　．　．

As the weather continued to warm, Jake played baseball nearly every day. If he and Joe couldn't find enough fellows for a game, they hit fly balls to each other or practiced their pitching. Jake and his friend had built a regulation mound by Railroad Avenue. Jake's only baseball was more tape than leather, but the boys still imagined they were in the big leagues. As Jake took his turn, Joe called an imaginary game from a catcher's crouch. "The bases are loaded with two outs in the bottom of the ninth. The count is three and two. Hubbell takes the sign and goes to the stretch. The Babe is waiting at the plate. . . ."

But whether Jake was playing ball, hiking to Mud Creek, or watching the horses in Bailey's corral, he couldn't stop worrying about his trip to Russia. Jake could tell that Mother was getting nervous, too. Lately, rather than singing and humming around the house, she'd been silent. One Saturday afternoon, Jake grinned when he saw Mother filling her scrub bucket. "You don't want to go to Russia either," he said.

"Why would you say that?" Mother frowned.

"You're cleaning again," Jake said.

"I like my house clean."

"But you already mopped the floor once this morning."

"Oh dear," Mother said.

"It was the same way after Grandma died," Maija said. "You had us cleaning all day long."

"You know me too well." Mother gave them both a hug. "Mrs. Koski's cousin told her that things are unsettled in Karelia. And I keep remembering how scary it was to leave Finland as a young girl." Mother shivered as though a cold wind had swept over her. "But we'll have to make the best of it. Jaakko, would you carry these things back to the basement? Our house is clean enough."

During the first week in May, the Co-op Store held a going-away party for Jake's family and the Salos, another couple who was relocating to Karelia. Ed Salo and Father had moved from the Upper Peninsula of Michigan to Minnesota together and gone to work for U.S. Steel. One winter when Salo was laid off by the mine, he started a sawmill. The mill did so well that by October 1929, he'd saved up enough money to buy a brand-new Buick. Salo took delivery of his car only a week before the stock market crashed.

Father teased Ed about driving a car that was a symbol of capitalism, yet he knew his friend was as dedicated to socialism as he was. Father helped at Salo's Mill on weekends, and Peter was thinking about going to work for Salo if times didn't improve.

Jake visited with Joe and his other Finntown friends during the party. "This is like Christmas and a wedding dance rolled into one," Joe said as he filled a punch glass and took his third handful of cookies from the table.

"It's more like a funeral to me," Jake said.

"You might have fun in Karelia," Joe said.

"Says who?" Jake picked up a roll, but he didn't feel like eating.

"I heard that Salo is bringing his Buick to Russia," Joe said. "Just think if he lets you drive it!" Salo's black Series 60 Dual Cowl Phaeton with its white sidewall tires and chrome bumpers and radiator was the envy of every boy on the Mesabi Range.

"Do you really think he'll ship his car all the way over there?" Jake asked.

"Sure —" Joe was cut short when an accordion player stepped forward and led the people in a rousing dance.

Late in the evening, a socialist leader from Duluth gave a speech, congratulating both families. "Follow these travelers in spirit," he said, "until you find the courage to commit your own hearts to the journey." He then presented Hudson's Bay blankets to Mrs. Salo and Mother.

As the audience applauded, Maija smiled, proud that

Father was getting the attention he deserved. Jake only hung his head.

People were just getting ready to go home when Peter elbowed Jake and pointed toward the door. "Look."

"It's Uncle Urho!" Jake said.

"We haven't seen him since that Fourth of July picnic in Alcott Park two summers ago," Peter said.

"Remember the look on Urho's face when Father announced he'd joined the Socialist Party?" Jake asked.

Peter nodded. "I thought they were going to get into a fistfight right in front of the bandstand."

Urho smiled as he wove through the crowd. Father didn't notice his brother until Urho tapped him on the arm. Father scowled. "Have you come to sell me a Bible for my trip?" Since Urho was a "church" Finn and Father a "Red" Finn, religion and politics were always at the heart of their quarrels.

"I didn't come here to fight." Urho took Father aside. "I only wanted to give you this." Jake was amazed to see Urho pull out a fifty-dollar bill. Since his uncle was a poor country farmer and part-time minister, it must have taken him many months to save the money.

"No," Father said. "I couldn't."

"Please," Urho said. "Save it for hard times. And no matter what they tell you, don't give up your American dollars or your passports. I've heard rumors about a Red broom from fellows who've come back from Russia. They say that once that broom begins to sweep, there'll be no escaping."

"Nonsense. I couldn't possibly take your —"

"Marta and I have talked this over. I've never asked you for a favor. But do this much" — he pressed the bill into Father's hand and waved toward Mother and the children — "if not for yourself, for them." Before Father could say another word, Urho shook Mother's and Maija's hands, and he clapped Peter and Jake on the back. "God's peace," he said, and then he was gone.

Jake expected Father to make a sarcastic comment about Urho's blessing, but he only stared toward the door.

Jake was about to ask Father what his uncle had meant by the Red broom sweeping, when the Co-op manager walked up to Father. "We're going to miss you, Arvid," he said. "If I was a few years younger, I'd be chasing off with you."

BON VOYAGE

Drink your milk, Maija." Father smiled. "It may be a long time before you have milk again." The same grin had been frozen on Father's face since the day he'd received the letter from Karelian Technical Aid.

Now that the morning of their departure had come, Jake tried to tell himself the journey would be no different than a vacation. But as he paced through the empty rooms of their rented house, he knew that it was foolish to pretend he would ever be coming home.

Getting ready to leave had been a constant rush. In addition to his schoolwork, Jake had helped Father and

Ed Salo disassemble the sawmill. Salo was shipping his equipment to Karelia, where he and Father would set it back up.

Salo was a thick-necked bull of a man who threw himself into his work. He was fond of saying, "Gabbing don't make sawdust." When Salo picked up a wrench to take off the first bolt, he said, "I sure hope we remember how to put this rig back together."

"Should I sketch the machinery first?" Jake asked.

"What's that?" Salo asked.

"Jake's a good drawer, Ed," Father said. "It might help us keep things straight if he drew a diagram."

"If you can do it quick," Salo said, digging out a sheet of paper. "You want me to pose, Jake?" He took off his cap and stood behind the big saw blade with his bald head shining.

"Get your face out of there." Father laughed.

After Jake made a diagram, they tagged and crated the equipment so it could be shipped to Lönnrot, the Russian logging town where both families had been assigned. The Karelian Aid director had promised Father he could move to Petrozavodsk as soon as the sawmill was running.

Jake was excited when he found out that Ed Salo really was sending his Buick to Karelia. On the day that Ed drove his car to Duluth, Jake and Father followed in their Model T truck. The old Ford sounded like a washing machine compared to the Phaeton's Inline 6 engine. When they arrived at the Duluth docks, Jake was impressed to see a dozen cars and trucks parked along with logging equipment, tools, and a tractor, that people had donated to Karelia. There was even a chicken incubator and a combine that a farmer had sent all the way from North Dakota.

Jake sat behind the wheel of the Buick and ran his hand over the plush seat. "It sure will be nice for you to have your car with you in Russia, eh, Mr. Salo?"

"We're headed for the north woods," Salo said. "A car like this won't do me no good up there."

"So you don't plan on driving it much?"

"I'll never even see it. I've donated it to the Karelian Machine Fund so it can be used for the good of all the people."

So much for driving the Buick, Jake thought.

Since the Makis only had a few dollars in their Co-op Credit Union account, they had to auction off their truck and all their furniture to pay for the steamship tickets. The night before the sale, Mother spent the evening cleaning the house and pacing. "Are you sure we're doing the right thing, Arvid?" she asked, running a dust cloth over the top of a dresser.

"You worry too much."

"But —"

"Would you stop beating a dead horse?" Father asked. "Either we leave this place or we let Peter's talent go to waste."

Peter surprised Jake by saying, "I don't want the whole family to move on account of me. I can get a job easily enough."

"It's not just for you." Father silenced Peter with his eyes. "Maija and Jake will have the opportunity to enroll in Petrozavodsk's finest Finnish school."

Mother sighed as she had all spring. "I suppose you're right, Arvid."

But on the morning of the auction, Mother stayed next door in Mrs. Koski's kitchen, weeping. Since Mother was usually so strong, Jake thought Father might change his mind. As they were carrying the furniture to the lawn and getting ready for the auctioneer, Jake said, "It's not too late for Peter and me to bring these things back inside."

"Is that your idea of being helpful?" Father's eyes sparked.

"No, sir," Jake said.

Maija smiled. "Can I help with anything, Father?"

Peter patted Jake on the shoulder. "We'll just have to look on this as an adventure, Hub. None of us kids have ever been farther than Duluth, and now we'll get to see the world."

By lunchtime, they'd sold everything that wouldn't fit into two wooden trunks and four backpacks. The only things Jake could cram into his pack other than his clothes were his baseball glove and ball, a hunting knife, a compass, and a cigar box full of baseball cards.

BY LAND AND BY SEA

Once the tickets were bought, Jake's family was left with only a few extra dollars, excluding Uncle Urho's emergency money. Mother was nervous about traveling with a nearly empty purse, but Father said, "We're going to the land of rubles. Our dollars won't mean a thing over there."

The Salos had left two weeks earlier because they were visiting relatives in Oulu, Finland, on their way to Russia. By the time the Makis boarded the train for New York, Father was so excited that he could barely sit down. "Are you ready for a bold new world?" he asked, clapping Peter on the shoulder.

"Let's just hope that world is ready for you, Father." Peter grinned.

Their cross-country trip was a blur of light and sound that took them roaring past the greening fields of the Midwest and over the bright Appalachian highlands, ending at last in New York's Grand Central Station. Jake would never forget the four-sided brass clock of the main concourse and the vaulted ceiling with its painted evening sky and gilded constellations.

After a week's stay in the Harlem Finn Hall, the Makis' departure from New York Harbor was a grand celebration. Hundreds of passengers clustered along the railing of the ship, calling good-bye. Father had talked to his comrades the night before and said, "Since the people call us Reds, let's not disappoint them," and he'd convinced everyone to wear red shirts and red sweaters.

Jake and his family jostled up the gangway and barely had time to find a place along the railing before the whistle blew. The crowd on shore waved red handkerchiefs, and flags waved as the ship pulled away from the pier. Then a chant rose up: "Long live the Soviet Union! Long live the Finnish Workers' Federation!"

The passengers on the ship responded by singing "The Internationale" — the workers' song. The chorus stayed strong as the ship headed for the open sea. Jake wanted to believe this voyage would take them to the land of opportunity that Father had promised, but all he could think about was his empty home back in Finntown and the unknown course that lay ahead.

After three days in London, they boarded an elegant ship, which took them across the Baltic Sea and through Germany's Kiel Canal. When Jake finally arrived on Russian soil, he saw two pictures that would remain forever etched in his mind. The first was the grand beauty of the Winter Palace, the former home of the Russian czars. Even as Jake admired the sweeping roof, the golden statues in the courtyard, and the ornate arched window frames, Father complained, "Can you believe such greed? Imagine the millions of peasants who suffered so this castle could be built."

"But you have to admit it's spectacular," Peter said.

"This monstrosity explains why the revolutionaries here have chosen to divide the riches among all men."

"I agree," Maija said.

The second image that confronted Jake was small and dark and everything the gilded palace was not. After the immigrants disembarked, they had to stand in line for three hours in the hot sun in front of a customs office, waiting for the inspectors.

Finally, a short man in a sweat-stained cap and uniform opened the door. The people were divided into two lines and forced to wait outside the building. When the Makis' turn came, it was hotter inside than it had been in the street.

The inspector tossed their clothes onto a dirty table. Jake cringed as the man's black fingernails brushed across his undershirt. And Mother frowned when ash flecks from the inspector's soggy cigarette fell into her trunk.

Jake looked at the couple in line beside them. As the second inspector reached for their suitcase, the man handed him a pack of cigarettes along with a five-dollar bill. The inspector smiled and slipped the package into his coat pocket. Then he waved the man and his wife through.

"Did you see that?" Jake whispered.

"What are you mumbling about now?" Father said, but by the time he turned, the couple was gone.

After the inspector finished pawing through the Makis' luggage, Father started to walk past him. But the man held up his hand and pointed for them to step aside.

For the next two hours the inspector checked several families through, but he never once looked their way. At lunchtime, he walked away without saying a word. Father said, "That little bureaucrat is going to get a piece of my mind when he comes back."

"Why don't we just catch a ship back to America?" Jake asked.

Before Father could snap at Jake, Mother said, "Perhaps he'll return in a better mood."

"He certainly can't be crabbier," Peter said.

When the door opened an hour later, Father marched forward.

"Be careful, Arvid," Mother said, stopping when she saw that a new man had been assigned to their line.

"My apologies, Mr. . . ." The man spoke in strongly accented but understandable English as he looked at Father's passport. "Mr. Maki, but delays are sometimes — how you say — inavoidable."

"Unavoidable," Father said. "Your apology is accepted."

"Yes, unavoidable." The man glanced at their papers

and asked what their destination was in the Soviet Union. Then he escorted the family to the doorway.

Jake stepped onto the wooden sidewalk, feeling better about Russia until he looked down. A man in a blacksmith's apron was lying in the dusty street, clutching a bottle of shaving lotion to his chest. Jake saw a picture of a reindeer on the label.

"We call it *poro rommi*," the inspector called through the half-open door. "That means 'reindeer rum.'"

"Why would anyone drink shaving lotion?" Jake asked. "Isn't it poison?"

"We have a word for the ones who've given up," the inspector said. "It's called *nichevo* and means that nothing matters."

The inspector tipped his cap and said, "Have a safe journey," then he stepped back inside.

As they shouldered their packs and started down the street, Peter looked back. "I sure feel sorry for that poor fellow."

"How can they leave a man lying in the gutter if this is a land where people work for the good of all?" Jake asked.

"There are weak folks in every country," Father said,

sounding like he was trying to convince himself. "Even socialists have to be strong enough to help themselves."

"How can Russia be so great if they have a special word for the men who've given up hope?" Jake asked.

"So, now you're an expert on international affairs," Father began. "I swear —"

Peter touched Father's arm and said, "We'd better hurry if we want to catch our train."

THE SLEEPING BEAR

On their way to board the train for Karelia, Jake saw ten times as many poor people in the streets of Leningrad as he had in New York. Jake waited for Father to comment on the filthy conditions, but he was too excited to see anything but his dream. "I can't believe we're finally here," he kept repeating.

"How far is it to our logging camp?" Maija asked.

"A three-day ride," Father said.

Soon they were bumping down the tracks in a dirty train car. The unsmiling passengers alternately dozed and lunched on smelly hunks of cheese and sausage. The wooden seats hurt Jake's back, and even Father admitted that the tracks needed repair.

The train stopped often, sometimes to pick up passengers and sometimes for no reason at all. Every station along the way was crowded with thin-faced Russians in tattered clothes. Many wore sandals sewn out of birch bark. Children and old people begged for food, but the passengers ignored them.

"Don't the peasants have houses?" Jake asked.

"The *Työmies* newspaper explained it all," Father said. "Those are kulaks whose farms have been taken by the government. The Russians punish greed instead of worshipping it like the Americans. Revolution is not always pretty, but as Lenin said, 'You can't make an omelet without breaking a few eggs.'"

After the fancy meals on the ship, Jake expected to see restaurants at the train stations, but there were only small stands selling bread and tea. At one stop Maija said, "Look, there's bread just like the recruiter promised."

Mother's eyes lit up when she saw the counter stacked with round black loaves. "That looks like the rye my mother baked back in Finland. The lean soils made for hearty grain."

"And it made for hearty people, too." Father took Mother's hand. "That's where you get your *sisu*."

Jake grinned. *Sisu* was a Finnish word that meant having the strength and courage to continue against all odds. Father often teased Mother about having *sisu* to spare.

When Father bought a loaf of bread, Mother's smile turned to a frown. "It feels a bit stale," she said, breaking off a piece.

Jake sniffed at the bread. "And it smells like vinegar," he said, swallowing a dry bite.

"Be thankful you're not marching into exile like those kulaks," Maija said.

"Your sister's right," Father said. "Besides, bread is bread." But his mouth was so dry that his words were muffled.

"Would you care for some water, Father?" Peter smiled, offering him a drink from the jar they'd been sharing.

Father took a swig. "Socialists aren't supposed to complain." He chuckled. "But I have to admit this bread tastes like it was made from sawdust."

To go along with the bread, Mother opened a can of fish. After everyone had taken a piece, a woman across from them, who was sharing a crust with her toddler, kept staring at Mother.

"I think she wants the can," Jake said. And when he handed it to the woman, she smiled and said, "*Spasibo*." Then she and her child took a corner of their bread and wiped the oil out of the can until they had polished the metal clean.

Later when Jake tried to sleep, he was haunted by the hungry eyes of that child. He stretched out on the wooden bench, but every time he dozed off, the train car shook or the engine blew its piercing whistle. Each time he woke, Father was still staring out the dark window.

Just before dawn, Jake gave up trying to sleep and sat up.

"It's just as the recruiter promised," Father whispered.

Jake nodded. He had to admit that the unspoiled wilderness was inspiring. The train passed clear streams, impenetrable tracts of tall pine, and open plains dotted with small farms.

"I feel like we've arrived on the shores of an undiscovered country," Father said. "I see why they call Russia a sleeping bear. Imagine the roar she'll make if she ever wakes up."

As Jake watched the soft rays of sunlight burn the mist from the dark-crowned trees, for the first time he could understand why people would seek such a place to fulfill their dreams.

THE LAND OF THE MIDNIGHT SUN

Three bone-jarring days later, their train arrived at Kem, a port city on the White Sea. After a night in a cramped hotel, the Makis, along with two other Finnish families, boarded a rickety bus that stank of diesel fuel. As they headed west, the driver, who spoke a dialect of Finnish that Jake could barely understand, told Father that Salo and his equipment had arrived the week before.

The other immigrants traveling to Lönnrot were the Salmis, a couple from Hancock, Michigan, and the Varpus, a family with two children from Astoria, Oregon. Though everyone was excited about their journey, Mr. Varpu complained before he even took his seat. "Where I come from, this rattletrap would have been hauled to the junk-yard long ago."

The ten-hour ride to the logging camp was dusty but scenic. As they chugged up a rocky hill, Peter pointed out the window. "Two men couldn't put their arms around those pines," he said.

Jake nodded, admiring the vast virgin forest.

Father said, "This is what Minnesota must have looked like before the timber barons raped the land."

"It was the same way in the Upper Peninsula," the Michigan man agreed.

But Mr. Varpu said, "We've got bigger trees in Oregon."

Late in the afternoon, the bus arrived at the village of Uhtua on the north shore of Lake Keskikuitti. "They say Uhtua supplies all the logging camps in central Karelia," Father said.

Jake couldn't believe this old-fashioned frontier town was a supply center. He could only see a couple two-story buildings along with a church, small school, granary, and store. A handful of log houses were scattered along the gravel road that led to the lake. An ancient, open-decked steamboat was tied to a pier.

The driver pulled up in front of a log store, and everyone but the Salmis, Varpus, and Makis left the bus. When Jake got up to stretch, the driver said, "Don't bother getting out. We'll be heading on to the Lönnrot Camp in a minute."

Mother brightened every time she heard the name of the camp. "Lönnrot!" she said to Father. "Can you imagine?"

"All Lönnrot did was write down an old poem," Father said.

"It wasn't just any poem, Arvid Maki." She turned to the children. "Elias Lönnrot traveled through Karelia a century ago. He listened to rune singers for many years before he wrote down his *Kalevala* epic."

"My father knew parts of it by heart," Mrs. Salmi said.

When they arrived at Lönnrot a half hour later, the driver announced that he was heading back to Uhtua. A stocky Russian man in a threadbare gray shirt greeted Father. "You must be Mr. Maki," he said. "My name is Victor Karlov." Karlov had a pockmarked nose and an untrimmed black beard that grew high up on his cheeks. He was accompanied by a short wolflike dog, who sat at his feet when he stopped. Karlov spoke the same Russian-accented Finnish as the bus driver. "Your quarters will be over there." The dark man waved toward a low log building, and the dog's ears stood up as he followed Karlov's hand with his eyes.

"This certainly is an improvement over the ore-stained streets of the Mesabi Range," Father said to Mother.

Jake knelt and called, "Here, boy," to the dog, but the animal stayed at Karlov's feet.

"Medved is a girl," Karlov said. Her coat was shiny black except for white patches that ran down her forehead and chest. When Jake stepped toward the dog, she let out a low growl.

"Medved won't hurt you, but she is suspicious of strangers." When the dog heard her name she stood up and arched her back. Then she looked over her shoulder at the newcomers and blinked her dark brown eyes like a movie star posing for a photographer.

"She's a real beauty," Father said.

"And she knows it," Karlov said.

Mother looked toward Keskikuitti. "What a lovely lake."

"Do you suppose the lake has pearls in it, Mother?" Maija asked. "Like you found in your village?"

The blue water was bordered by pine ridges and lichen-coated rocks. Scattered patches of white sand broke up the gray shoreline. "I wonder how far across it is," Jake said.

"It must be wider than Lake Superior," Maija said.

"That would be an exaggeration," a voice boomed behind them, making Maija squeal, "but this little pond is more than sixty miles from end to end." It was Ed Salo. "Long time no see, Arvid." He pumped Father's arm.

Karlov turned to Father. "I will allow Mr. Salo to show you the grounds." But when he bowed and turned to leave, he stopped. "Would you look at that?"

Karlov's dog had walked up to Maija, and Maija was petting her. "I can't believe it," Karlov said. "Medved's never taken to anyone that quickly."

When Jake tried petting Medved, she laid back her ears and growled. "See what I mean?" Karlov said.

Maija stuck out her tongue at Jake.

Karlov was still shaking his head as he walked toward an old farmhouse across the road. Medved trotted at his side for a moment and then loped toward the woods.

"That man is creepy." Maija shuddered.

"Maija!" Mother said. "Behave yourself."

"That's all right, Mrs. M." Salo lowered his voice. "If you ask me, Mr. Karlov is a bit of a cold fish."

"I will not allow my children to be impolite," Mother said.

"Of course not," Salo said.

"So what about that tour?" Father asked.

"You can see the whole place from right here."

"This is everything?" Jake asked.

"I admit it's not much," Salo said. "But there'll be lots of timber for us to mill, as I'm sure you noticed on your ride in. In front of you is the bunkhouse, and just beyond, the storehouse and workshop. That farmhouse across the road is where Karlov — otherwise known as the 'cold fish' — stays." He grinned at Maija.

"Would you please not encourage her?" Mother scolded.

"One interesting thing is that abandoned gristmill." Salo pointed across the clearing toward a stone ruin. "It would be a perfect site to generate electricity."

"There's no electricity here?" Maija asked.

"Nope," Salo said. "But we've got some fine kerosene lamps, and it'll be your job to see that the globes stay polished."

Maija wrinkled her nose.

"Where are you setting up the sawmill?" Father asked.

"Karlov wants it between here and the river," Salo said.

"That's mighty low ground. Why did they pick such an out-of-the-way place for a mill?"

"There's an export lumber company in Kem," Salo said, "but they want this operation to saw lumber for the local villages."

Father smiled when he saw that the machinery was covered with canvas tarps. "It looks like you haven't got much of a start. Did you lose Jake's diagram?"

"No, I've got it right here." Salo pointed to his shirt pocket. "But we've only been here a few days, and —" Salo paused to make sure that Karlov was out of earshot. "The real problem is Karlov. He's supposed to be in charge, but he never wants to make a decision. And he jabbers a mix of Finn and Rusky that I can't make heads or tails of."

"How would you know whether he's talking Finnish or Russian when all you speak is English?" Father laughed.

"It's all a jumble to me," Salo said. "A few other Russians have stopped by to help, but nobody seems to care."

Father nodded. "The language I can handle. But we've seen a bit of that not-caring attitude ourselves." He turned to Peter. "What did the inspector back in Leningrad call it?"

Peter usually had a perfect memory for words, but Jake remembered first. "*Nichevo*," Jake said, recalling the black-smith and his reindeer rum. "It means that a man has given up hope."

"Well, I've seen about all the *nichevo*" — Salo pronounced

it "nachavoo" — "I can stand. But now that Arvid's here, we'll show these fellows how to saw wood, right?" He punched Father's arm. "In the meantime, I'll help you unpack your stuff."

Mr. Salo led them to the log barracks. "Watch your noggin, Peter," he said, opening the rough plank door. "There ain't much clearance for tall fellows around here."

Before Jake stepped through the doorway, his nose burned from the smell of wood smoke and boiled cabbage.

Mrs. Salo hugged Mother. "Welcome to Lönnrot, Annikki," she said. As Mother scanned the dark log walls, Mrs. Salo said, "I'm sorry it's not very fancy."

"All a man needs is a roof over his head," Father said.

But Mother looked worried. "Are there bedrooms?"

"The barracks is just two rooms, the community kitchen and the bunk room back here." She led them through a low doorway.

"It was built for loggers," Mrs. Salo said.

Jake stared at the crude sleeping room. It looked worse than a trapper's shack. Strips of bark clung to the log walls, and the grimy wooden floor was riddled with holes from the spiked boots of loggers. Blankets draped over sagging ropes divided the room.

"The blankets offer a bit of privacy," Mrs. Salo said.

Jake couldn't believe four families would be sleeping here! Mother was staring, too. "I know it's not much, Annikki, but —" Mrs. Salo stopped suddenly. "Who am I fooling?" she whispered. "This is an awful way to live. If I had my way, we'd —"

"So what do you think of our little log hotel?" Mr. Salo said as he and Father entered the room. Salo saw his wife dabbing her eyes with the sleeve of her dress. "Isn't dinner about ready?"

"Yes, dear," Mrs. Salo said, pressing Mother's hand as she turned. "It will only be a minute."

The meal of cabbage soup and sour black bread left Jake's stomach rumbling. When they were done, Salo said, "How about a stroll? You folks won't want to miss your first northern sunset."

Salo led the way to the shore of the lake. Though it was ten o'clock, Jake was amazed that the sun was just beginning to set.

"Should we try a Midsummer's bonfire?" Salo asked.

Jake was hoping he could go to bed, but Father said, "I can't think of a more perfect way to celebrate our new beginning."

Later, as the flames fell to embers, the families took turns telling about the hard-rock mines, stump farms, and lumber towns they'd left behind. Mr. Salmi added green branches to smoke away the mosquitoes, and the smell of burnt birch tickled Jake's nose.

Just before midnight, the sun was an orange ball blazing above the water. As bursts of color washed the starlit sky, Father asked Peter to get out his clarinet. Jake could tell that the men were uneasy about an amateur concert, but once Peter began playing, everyone sat in rapt attention. When Peter played a folk ballad about a young girl who seeks her true love, the whole group joined in the chorus, their voices mingling with the smoke and drifting out over the black waters of the lake:

> *I'll know my darling by her step.*
> *As mist I'll go,*
> *as sparks I'll speed,*
> *as flame I'll fly,*
> *to stand by her fair side.*

By the time Peter finished playing, the sun had begun to rise. Everyone sat in silence and watched the wonder of a new day dawning at midnight. Jake admired the perfect quiet. No red mine dust. No traffic noise. No glaring city lights. Perhaps this would be a workers' paradise after all.

However, Jake's mood soured only a few minutes later when he crawled into the top bunk and something scrunched beneath him. "What's in these mattresses?" he asked.

Peter, who was sleeping in the bunk next to him, reached under his blanket. "It feels like straw," he said.

"Haven't they heard of feather beds?" Jake tried to flatten the lumps, but the straw kept poking him.

Jake expected Father to scold him, but he and Maija were both so allergic to the straw they couldn't stop coughing and sneezing.

The other families were quiet except for the grumpy man from Oregon. "Do they think we're cattle?" Mr. Varpu spoke loud enough for the whole room to hear. "Why not just stick us in a barn!"

Mother leaned over Maija's bunk and squeezed her hand. "Breathe slow and steady, dear," she whispered.

But Maija kept wheezing like she had a bad cold. "I want to go home," Maija cried.

"I second the motion," Jake said.

"Did you expect a castle?" Father coughed. "We're here to do the people's work. The recruiter warned us that this would be a test — not some capitalist vacation."

A NEW DAY

The next morning, Jake was so tired that his whole body ached. But the moment he saw Maija, he stopped feeling sorry for himself. Her eyes were nearly swollen shut, and her breathing was raspy. Father looked just as miserable, though Jake knew he would never admit it.

When Jake climbed down from his bunk, he noticed clusters of red marks on his arms. "Did you scratch yourself in your sleep?" Mother asked, touching his arm gently.

"I forgot to warn you, Annikki." Mrs. Salo stepped from behind her curtain. "We have a few bugs."

"Dear me." Mother frowned. "Bedbugs?"

Mrs. Salo nodded.

"I thought the straw was pricking me," Jake said, shivering at the thought of bugs biting him in his sleep.

"That's what the borax is for." Mrs. Salo pointed to the legs of the bunk beds. Each post was standing in a cap filled with white powder. "It's supposed to help, but they say the only way to get rid of the bugs is to freeze them out in the winter."

"What would the wilderness be without a little wildlife?" Father tried to joke, but his throat sounded scratchy.

Just then, Jake heard a sharp bark coming from the front door. Still trying to focus his sleep-swollen eyes, he made his way through the kitchen and opened the door. Karlov's dog, Medved, was sitting on her haunches, and she'd laid a freshly killed squirrel on the steps. "Are you offering us breakfast?" Jake grinned at the dog, but when he stepped toward her, she growled. "I get it," Jake said. "You've come to see your friend."

"Maija," Jake called. "You've got company."

When Maija stepped into the doorway, Medved barked happily and picked up the bloody squirrel.

"Yuck," Maija said. "Go home."

Disappointed, the dog lowered her ears and trotted back toward the farmhouse, but she left her prize behind.

Breakfast was thick black porridge. Maija frowned at her bowl and said, "Why is my cereal black?"

"Maybe we should fry you some squirrel?" Peter grinned.

"Stop it," Maija groaned.

"The cereal is buckwheat," Mr. Salo said. "If you give it a chance, I think you'll like it."

Though Jake had the same doubts as his sister, he found the cereal had a hearty flavor.

"Food is food," Father said. "When you live in Russia, you should eat like the Russians." Then Father took a big drink of coffee and almost spit it back into his cup. "What's this?" He looked at the brown liquid. "It tastes like burnt silage."

"Coffee is hard to come by," Mrs. Salo said, "so we brew up roast barley. The local folks all drink it."

"It's a poor excuse for coffee."

"Father?" Maija asked. "If we're going to eat like the Russians, shouldn't we drink like them, too?"

When everyone at the table laughed, Father grinned, too. "Yes, Maija, you're right." He raised his cup. "To the Russians." He took another swallow and tried not to grimace.

As soon as breakfast was done, Father said, "We'd

better get started on the mill." He turned to the men. "You fellows ready to get your hands dirty?" Before they stepped outside, Father pulled a cap out of his pack and tossed it to Peter. "That sun's going to be mean today," he said. "Us light-skinned fellows better keep our heads covered." Though Father and Peter turned blotchy red if they spent too much time outside, Jake and Mother and Maija got deep tans.

All the men but Mr. Varpu hurried to catch up with Father. "Aren't you coming?" Salo called to Varpu.

"My family and I are heading home," he said.

"What?" Salo stopped.

"Do I have to spell it out? We're going back to where people sleep on mattresses instead of swamp grass."

"Suit yourself," Father said, turning up the hill and walking fast as he always did. "Let's see what this site has to offer."

Jake followed the men. As much as he disliked Mr. Varpu, Jake couldn't help but think he was making a smart choice.

While the men were examining the slope of the ground, Karlov walked down from the farmhouse. He looked as stiff and unfriendly as he had the night before. Medved, who'd been exploring the woods, ran over to greet her master. But as soon as Karlov stopped to talk with the men, the dog trotted to the bunkhouse and barked until Maija came out to see her.

"Good morning, Mr. Karlov," Father said. "We've been studying the lay of the land."

"Yes?" Karlov's bushy eyebrows crinkled into a frown.

"And we all agree it's too low for a sawmill."

"But the Party Planning Committee selected this site."

"In that case, the Party is wrong," Father said.

Mr. Salmi coughed. "Folks usually don't question the Party like that, Arvid."

"Everyone makes mistakes. Even the Party," Father said. "This will be a quagmire the first time it rains."

Karlov stared at the equipment. Mr. Salmi scraped the ground nervously with the toe of his boot.

"So what do you say?" Salo said, forgetting that Karlov couldn't speak English. "We don't want to haul my mill eight thousand miles and set it up in a mud hole, do we?"

Karlov turned to Father. "What would you suggest?"

"There's well-drained gravel up by the road," Father said. "Trucks and wagons would have no trouble hauling in logs."

To Jake's surprise, Karlov said, "Very well. We will try what you suggest. However, be advised that if this plan does not succeed, the blame will be yours."

54

"Just tell your boss that you ran into a stubborn bunch of Finns that didn't know how to follow orders."

"If it were only that simple, Mr. Maki."

A short while later, Karlov returned with a hay wagon pulled by a tired-looking plow horse.

"Don't you have a pickup truck on your farm?" Father asked.

"This is not my farm," Karlov said. "I live near a town called Paanajärvi. The Party assigned me to this project."

"Well, a wagon will be better than carrying the stuff on our backs," Father said.

The crew of Finns smiled as they piled the materials on the wagon. Along with Salo's equipment, the Russians had delivered a pile of rusty sheet metal roofing and a half keg of nails.

"Let's not load her too heavy," Father said. "That old gray mare" — he nodded at the horse — "ain't what she used to be."

Salo pointed to himself. "And this old gray Finn ain't what he used to be neither."

Father grinned at Peter and Jake. "It's good to finally be doing the people's work, eh, boys?" he said, sliding a piece of channel iron onto the wagon bed. "And now that Karlov has seen things our way, we can do this job right. It won't be like it is in America, where the bigwigs are always telling you what to do."

Jake had to admit that it felt fine to flex his muscles and soak in the sun of this clear northern land.

While the men worked on the mill, the women battled the bedbugs. They aired out the mattress ticks and filled them with fresh straw, and then they washed the floors of the bunkhouse with soapy water and polished them with white river sand.

When the men returned for lunch, Salo said, "I hope you ladies gave our bedbugs proper notice before you evicted them."

"I'll give you notice to stop wagging that tongue, Ed Salo." Riita Salo waved a wooden spoon at her husband.

It felt strange for Jake to go to bed when the sky was still bright, but he was looking forward to a good night's rest. Yet he'd barely settled under his blanket when the familiar itching began. As Jake dug at his forearm, he heard Peter slap himself in the other bunk. "It looks like our wildlife is still with us," Father said, sneezing hard.

"And the new hay tickles my nose even worse," Maija answered with a sneeze of her own.

"And I was hoping I could get out our good white sheets," Mother said, sounding like she was about to cry.

Only ten days later the men had the mill assembled and roofed. The hardest job was ripping the timbers by hand with a long whipsaw. "I can understand why they wanted a sawmill." Salo grinned. "I haven't whipsawed lumber since I was Jake's age."

Once the men mounted the big Minneapolis Moline tractor engine on the saw rig, one pull of a lever started the fifty-four-inch blade whirling. However, when Father rolled the first log onto the saw carriage, it tipped sideways as soon as Salo released the clutch. "What in the devil's wrong now?" he said.

Jake looked at his sketch and said, "I think we need to turn those metal teeth."

"These dogs, you mean?" Salo knelt down and checked the teeth that were supposed to pull the log forward. "I believe Squirt is right, boys. Hand me that wrench."

"I told you he was a good drawer," Father said.

On the next try, Salo ripped off a straight slab of wood, and the fellows cheered. "Good work, Hub," Peter said.

Only a few minutes later, their practice log had been

transformed into a pile of lumber. Salo took a deep breath and smiled. "Doesn't that fresh pine smell good?"

Father turned to Karlov. "So when do you expect our first load of logs to arrive?"

"That is hard to say."

"Aren't you the boss?" When Father raised his voice, Medved growled. The dog's dark eyes, divided by the white patch down her forehead, made her look like she was wearing a mask.

"Sit." Karlov snapped his fingers and the dog quieted. "We'd planned on using a tugboat to pull the logs to this shore, but the boat has been delayed."

When Salo saw Father's disgusted look he asked, "What's he saying, Arvid?"

As Father translated, Salo's brow creased. "You mean to tell me we've built a mill that he has no way to supply?"

Karlov shrugged his shoulders and spoke to Father. "It is out of my hands."

Father shook his head. "Why is every blessed thing in this country out of everyone's hands?"

As Karlov walked off, Jake said, "We could always go back home, you know."

"We are home." Father glared.

MEDVED'S MISSION

Whenever Father asked Karlov about the prospects for getting more logs, he always said, "It's only a matter of time."

"How much time?" Father asked. "A thousand years?"

Salo was even more irritated by the poor planning. As the weeks stretched on, he asked, "How are we supposed to build a new world over here when no one is in charge?"

Peter spent most of his spare time practicing his clarinet, but Jake often talked him into playing catch during the afternoon. Sports came to Peter as easily as schoolwork did, and he had excelled at both baseball and basketball in junior high school. Jake even carved a bat out of a birch stick so he and Peter could take turns hitting fly balls and grounders up in Karlov's field.

Maija played sometimes, and she improved rapidly at both her catching and throwing. One day she chased a line drive into the woods. When Jake trotted over to help her find the ball, Maija was standing beside a rock at the edge of a berry patch, staring.

"Where's the ball?" Jake called.

"Look," Maija whispered.

A few yards away, a bear cub rustled in the bushes. Jake had seen black bears in Minnesota, but this one was a cinnamon color.

"He's a cute little fellow." Jake spoke quietly.

Suddenly Jake heard a loud huff and the sound of teeth chomping together. He turned. A huge brown bear was charging them.

Maija screamed, and Jake grabbed her hand. "Run!" he yelled.

Just then, a sharp bark came from behind them, and a black-and-white blur streaked toward the bear. It was Medved. The bear rose on her hindquarters, standing taller than a man. One swipe of the long, curved claws would rip Medved apart.

With a snarl, the bear lunged at Medved, but the dog

darted to the left and circled behind the animal. Barking in a high, frantic pitch that Jake had never heard, Medved nipped the bear on the back of the leg. The bear roared and spun around, but the dog dodged behind her and bit her other leg.

"Let's go." Jake tugged at Maija's hand. But he stopped when he heard chuckling behind him. It was Karlov. He and Peter had run up the hill. "Don't worry," Karlov said, "Medved will keep her at bay."

"That little dog?" Peter asked.

"She's a Karelian bear dog. That's why I call her Medved — short for *Medvedchik*, or 'bear keeper,' in Russian. Those dogs have been bred to hunt bears since the days of the Vikings."

"She's got her on the run already," Peter said as they watched the bear retreat into the woods. Medved stayed close behind, darting from side to side faster than Jake had ever seen a dog move and barking on a piercing, high note the whole time.

"You can't find a fiercer hunting dog," Karlov said.

When Maija finally spoke, her voice trembled. "I didn't think bears got that big."

"That was only a little she-bear — no more than three hundred pounds, I'd guess," Karlov said. "The big males can be twice that size. Russian bears are first cousins to your American grizzlies."

Maija's eyes widened.

"I've seen them taller than the eave of my house." Karlov smiled as Medved trotted back and licked Maija's hands.

From that day forward, Maija refused to go near the field. Without a helper to fetch the balls, Jake and Peter played baseball less often. Jake missed baseball even more when he got a letter from Joe Santelli reporting on the All-Star Game. Jake had sent Joe his address two months before, and he couldn't figure out why it had taken him so long to write back until he saw the letter. It had already been opened by someone, probably a government censor. The dirty fingerprints on the envelope reminded Jake of the customs inspector in Leningrad.

> *Dear Jake,*
>
> *Thanks for your letter. After reading about your bunkhouse, I've decided that I would like to have a souvenir from Russia. Suppose you could mail me one of those bedbugs? Ha! Ha!*
>
> *Seriously, I hope that everything is okay over there. Things are going good in Finntown, except my big mouth*

got me in trouble the other day. I'd been doing a little boxing with the guys in the gym. I was holding my own until I sparred with Frankie Camden. I made the mistake of saying, "Let's see what you got, Frankie." Next thing I knew, they were using smelling salts to wake me up. I've still got a fat lip and a loose tooth. I'm sticking with baseball from now on.

Speaking of baseball, I listened to the second annual All-Star Game on the radio, and it was just as exciting as last year. Remember when the Babe smacked that homer in the bottom of the third? This year, your boy Carl Hubbell was the hero. He used his screwball to strike out five of the greatest players in the game in a row: Ruth, Gehrig, Foxx, Simmons, and Cronin.

Write and let me know how Salo's mill is going. You guys will probably be as rich as the Virginia & Rainy Lake Lumber Company pretty soon.

Your buddy,
Joe

Jake grinned when he read about Joe's boxing with Camden.

"What's so funny?" Peter asked.

Jake handed his brother the letter. Peter smiled until he got to the part about Salo's mill making them rich. "We're so rich that we eat black porridge every day." Peter shook his head. "Being that the Virginia mill used to saw a half million feet of lumber every day, I'd say we've got a long way to go."

Along with Jake's chores at Lönnrot, shopping became a daylong labor. Once each month, they borrowed Karlov's cart and rode to the old-fashioned general store in Uhtua. Bins, crocks, and barrels held flour, salt, and sugar (which was in short supply). Mother sewed sacks out of cloth to hold the loose items, and she brought milk home in used vodka bottles.

Their diet of bread and cabbage soup left Jake craving fruit. If only he could sink his teeth into a fresh apple or a pear. He kept thinking back to the big table of food the ladies had laid out at their going-away party. One night, Jake even dreamed that Mother had given him a big plate piled with green beans, but Maija grabbed it away before he could take a bite.

ALPHABET SOUP

With the coming of autumn, Lake Keskikuitti was clouded with fog each morning. Yet logs rarely showed up at the mill. Salo and Father even volunteered to do their own logging, but Karlov said, "You've been assigned as mill workers, not loggers."

By October, Salo had reached the end of his patience. One morning at breakfast, he said, "Riita and I are heading home."

"But this sawmill was your life," Father said.

"I can put together another mill easy enough," Salo said. "Or maybe I'll go back to the mines."

"There's bound to be problems when folks are trying to put a whole new system in place," Father said.

"We've given it chance enough, Arvid."

Father couldn't hide his disappointment over Salo's departure. The first hint came on the day after Salo left. Father stood up in the middle of breakfast and dumped his barley coffee into the sink. "You'd think a fellow could at least get a decent cup of java around here." Then he walked outside.

Later that same day, Father asked Karlov, "When will I be transferred to Petrozavodsk? The recruiter promised that Peter could try out for the orchestra."

"My orders show you as a mill worker," Karlov said, "and I've heard nothing to contradict that."

"How can I mill lumber without logs?"

Karlov shrugged his shoulders. "You could try writing to Party headquarters."

"I applied for Party membership before I left America, and I still haven't heard a thing."

"The government moves slowly," Karlov said. "And being in the American Communist Party doesn't guarantee admission."

"How do they expect to build a new world over here, when everyone is sitting on their hands?" Father said.

The next morning, Father wrote a letter to Moscow requesting a transfer to Petrozavodsk.

"We could always return home, Arvid," Mother said.

"That sounds good to me," Jake said. "Why stay if Karlov's never going to deliver any timber?"

"And who asked you?" Father said.

"I think it's nice here." Maija smiled.

"Miss Perfect would."

"Be nice, Jaakko," Mother said.

During the slow times at the mill, Jake and Peter explored the lakeshore and the woods. Medved often accompanied them on their hikes, but rather than staying nearby, she ran wide circles around the boys, disappearing for up to a half hour at a time.

One day Peter said, "Do you realize what that dog is doing?"

"Being bad company?"

"She's guarding us," Peter said. "Who knows how many bears she's chased away?"

As much fun as it was to hike and fish, Jake was homesick for Finntown, where he knew Joe and his buddies would be playing football. At thirteen, Jake had been looking forward to trying out for the seventh-grade team.

Jake was so bored that he enjoyed helping at the mill

when logs did come in. Mother must have read his mind, for one day she said, "I looked into enrolling you children in the Uhtua school, but you'd have to board over a week at a time."

"We sure don't want to live in Uhtua," Jake said.

"That's why I'm thinking of giving you Finnish lessons myself," Mother said. "Then you'll have a head start when we move to Petrozavodsk and you enroll in the Finnish school."

"You mean *if* we move to Petrozavodsk," Jake said.

Since Jake spoke Finnish, he thought that writing it would be easy. And he remained confident when Mother explained that there were no articles — a's, an's, or the's — in Finnish to worry about.

"So I don't have to say 'a dog' or 'the dog'?"

"Correct," Mother said. "Finns just say 'dog.' And Finnish verbs are easier, too. Instead of saying 'I will go,' you just say 'I go.'"

But once Mother showed the children how to write, her lessons got complicated. An easy word like "English" became *Englannin kieli* in Finnish. And though the spelling of numbers started out simply, with "one, two, three" as *yksi, kaksi, kolme*, "forty-eight" in Finnish was *neljäkymmentäkahdeksan*!

But as hard as the spelling was, noun case forms were even more complicated. "The spelling of a place name changes depending on its use," Mother said.

"How can that be?" Jake said.

"For instance, there is a pretty town on the coast of Finland called Oulu. If you're from Oulu, you say *Olen Oulusta*, but if you want to say you live in Oulu, you say *Asan Oulussa*."

"This gives me a headache," Maija said.

"And if you're traveling to Oulu, you say *Menen Ouluun*."

Even Peter was frowning now.

"Let's go back to spelling numbers," Jake said. "At least that makes sense."

A WINTER
OF DISCONTENT

As winter approached, Jake found himself longing for the Mesabi Range. He imagined the big red ore pit east of Chestnut Street and the rock terraces of the mine dumps beyond. He saw the cattle on Sauntry Hill, the horse corral at Bailey's Mill, and the globed streetlamps on Fifth Avenue.

When the lake in Lönnrot froze, Jake enjoyed zinging stones across the clear ice. But he had to promise to stay near shore because Mother was deathly afraid of the ice. She often told about a minister of her village in the 1700s, who had fallen through the ice and drowned, along with his wife and two children. When Mother was fishing one summer, she pulled up the dead minister's Bible. Thinking of that cold book still gave her nightmares.

Jake stared through the magical ice window into the shallows. He watched the light-dappled minnows swim across the bottom. He studied the clam trails and the weeds that stood perfectly still.

Once the cold weather settled in, Mother's Hudson's Bay blanket became her most prized possession. "It would be more homey if we could use our good sheets," she said, "but it's impossible to keep this place clean."

As a Minnesotan, Jake was used to short winter days, but by mid-December the sun was up for less than four hours each day. Even Peter, who rarely complained, found the long gray twilight depressing. One evening, he said, "I'm spending so much time under a kerosene lamp, I feel like my skin is turning yellow."

"There's always the moonlight if you care for something brighter," Mother tried to joke, but tears came to her eyes.

"Don't cry, Mother," Peter said, squeezing Mother's hand.

"I'm sorry," Mother said. "But it's so dark all the time."

"Let me play a tune to brighten things up," Peter said, reaching for his clarinet case.

■ ■ ■

Father spent the brief daylight keeping his saw blade sharp for logs that rarely came. Each week he wrote to Moscow, repeating his request for a transfer to Petrozavodsk. The first few times he chose his words with care. But after a while, he copied the same letter over, adding a different greeting at the top, such as DEAR MR. BUREAUCRAT or IS ANYONE THERE?

"Shouldn't you be more polite, Arvid?" Mother said.

Mr. and Mrs. Salmi both nodded their heads, but Father said, "What's the difference when no one reads them?"

Later that afternoon, Father was tinkering with the saw rig when Karlov walked down the hill. As usual, Medved came along, and she barked until Maija appeared.

"So why doesn't anyone answer my letters?" Father asked.

Karlov shrugged. "Moscow is a long way away," he said. "And things are mixed up in the government right now."

"That's no news." Father bent to adjust a tension bolt.

"I've received word that Sergei Kirov has been assassinated."

"The Party Secretary?" Father set down his wrench. "I read that he was doing a fine job."

"There had been talk that Kirov would succeed Stalin one day." Karlov showed rare emotion as he spoke. "Though Stalin is mounting a campaign to hunt down his killers, it doesn't add up."

"In what way?"

"Kirov was shot at the Leningrad headquarters, just after five bodyguards had escorted him into the building."

Before Father could ask another question, Karlov whistled to Medved and walked away.

Jake looked at Father. "Was he trying to say that the Party killed one of its own leaders?"

"Who knows what he means?" Father reached for his wrench. "Help me with this bolt."

Mother was frightened by the news, but Father only teased her. "No one's shot at us lately."

"Seriously, Arvid." Mother lowered her voice so Maija couldn't hear. "I've been thinking it might be wiser, with the mill not working out and all, for us to go back to the Range."

"We've got to be patient."

When Mother only sighed, Jake spoke up. "I thought you were the one who was tired of waiting."

Before Father could scold him, Mother said, "That's enough, Jaakko."

Karlov finally brought Father good news. "Loggers north of the village are building ice roads for horse-drawn sleds," he said. "We'll soon be giving your equipment a test."

"It's not my equipment," Father said. "It's Salo's."

"Salo? Maki?" Karlov smiled a rare smile. "What's the difference when the people's work calls?"

The men made quick work of the first few loads of logs. Father shouted, "Fine music, eh, boys?" over the whine of the saw blade. The scent of pine pitch filled the air as Jake and Peter tossed the slab wood aside and piled the freshly sawn lumber.

But Father grew impatient when the loggers couldn't keep up with the mill. During the down times, the men kept busy building a log sauna by the shore, expanding the workshop, and making new cabinets for the camp kitchen out of hand-planed birch.

Two good things happened with the arrival of the cold. One was the end of the bedbugs. On the first subzero night, Mother and Mrs. Salmi gave the bunkhouse a Russian–style fumigation by letting the fires die out. Then they opened all the windows, and everyone slept in Karlov's hay barn. "You'd think he'd invite us into his house," Father said as he and Maija began to sneeze.

74

"I'd rather sneeze than be near that creepy man," Maija said.

"Speak of your elders with respect." Mother sighed.

The second good thing was Jake's idea. Father had expected bonus pay from the mill, but with the small number of logs they were sawing, he was barely making enough money to pay for their food. "I'm afraid we're not going to have Christmas this year," he warned. "But as true socialists, we should replace Christmas with a Father Frost celebration at New Year's anyway."

Jake came up with a gift idea when he noticed the leftover lumber from Father's cabinetmaking. "What kind of wood are skis made out of?" he asked Father.

"Hickory usually."

"Would birch do?"

"What are you driving at?"

"It might be fun to make everyone skis for Christmas."

"That's a grand idea. And it would fill our slack times."

The next day while Peter was practicing his clarinet and Mother and Maija were working in the kitchen, Father asked Jake, "Would you mind helping me up at the mill?"

"Sure," Jake said as Father gave him a wink.

Father chose the wood carefully for each pair of skis. "It's important to use straight-grained stock for strength, and you always want to shape skis with the bark side down."

"How did you learn all that?"

"I made my first skis out of barrel staves. Then when I was your age, my grandpa showed me how to build a proper pair."

Only three days later, Jake and Father had the first two skis shaped and sanded. "What do you think?" Father asked.

"They look real," Jake said, running his hand over the white wood. "But what about the curved tips?"

"We'll make a bending jig after we finish the other pairs. Then we can steam them in the sauna."

During the month before Christmas, Jake and Father bent the ski tips, waterproofed the wood with pine tar, and made binding straps out of old harness leather. They also cut saplings for ski poles and wove "baskets" for the tips out of willow and leather.

When Christmas finally came, everyone was excited by their new skis, but Father had an even bigger surprise for Mother. It arrived the day after Christmas, tied on top of the bus from Kem. When Father looked out the window, he said, "Santa may be a little late, but he's found his way here at last."

"Whatever do you mean?" Mother asked.

To Mother's surprise, Father had arranged for their double bed to be shipped all the way from America. "I set it up with Eino Koski before we left."

"How sweet of you, Arvid." Mother smiled. "This will be a huge improvement over that straw tick."

Though the bedsprings had rusted, the brass headboard and mattress were in excellent condition.

During New Year's, several strangers came to visit the bunkhouse. Most of the people were from Uhtua, but one curious couple came all the way from Haikola. "If it wouldn't be an imposition, Mrs. Maki," Karlov said, "these folks would like to see the cupboards that Arvid built."

"Surely they can't be that special?" Mother asked.

"Built-in cupboards are a new idea in Russia."

Jake noticed that while the visitors did admire Father's cabinets, they seemed more anxious to peek into the bunk room and whisper to each other. When Jake overheard someone saying "American bed," he told Mother.

Once Mother learned that people were coming to see her scandalous double bed — a rarer thing than cupboards in Russia — she said, "I think it's time we put our tours to an end."

During the second week in January, a cold snap hit

Lönnrot. One night the temperature dropped to fifty-six below zero. Peter laughed when Jake tried skiing the next morning and his skis only squeaked to a stop on the frozen snow.

But as long as the temperature stayed at ten or twenty below, Jake rarely missed a day in the woods or on the lake. Sometimes he and Peter skied all the way to Uhtua, timing their return with the afternoon moonrise. "Last one back is a capitalist," Peter called as the brothers raced over the star-flecked snow. If Jake managed to pass Peter with a hard sprint at the end, Peter only laughed. "Good job, Hub. I'm going to have to spend less time sitting around with my clarinet."

Once Father convinced Maija that the bears were hibernating, she enjoyed her skis, too. She skied across Karlov's field, and Medved sometimes pulled her giggling down the road, using a harness that Karlov had rigged for hauling firewood.

Mother continued to tutor the children in Finnish, and as word spread of Father's fine skis, several men from Uhtua placed orders.

In early March, a stranger interrupted their lunch. "May I speak with Mr. Maki?" he asked. The man had an American accent, and he was holding a pair of skis in his hand.

"I'm Arvid Maki," Father said.

"Did you make these?" He showed Father the skis.

"Yes." Father nodded. "Is there some problem?"

"No, not at all." The man took off his cap. "Allow me to introduce myself. My name is Karl Ranta. I am a foreman at a ski factory. One of my coworkers brought me these skis. When I saw the design, I had to meet the man who'd made them."

Father smiled. "Why don't you take off your coat and have a seat?"

Before Mother could finish pouring a cup of tea for Mr. Ranta, the two men had plunged into a discussion of ski making. As Father explained how he chose the proper wood, Ranta nodded. "But what about your wax?" Ranta asked. "I didn't recognize the mixture."

"We made do with pine tar and candle wax, but back home I blended pine tar, bear grease, beeswax, and deer tallow."

"I see." Mr. Ranta looked at Father. "How would you like to work in our factory?"

"A ski factory might be interesting, but I am supposed to be transferred to a city called Petrozavodsk."

Ranta laughed. "That's where the Gylling Ski Factory is."

"They told us about Edvard Gylling at our summer

meetings in Mesaba Park," Father said. "It must be a fine operation if he's behind it."

With a handshake, Father agreed to accept a position in the ski factory. The Makis would finally be moving to Petrozavodsk.

As Ranta got up to leave he said, "I'll start the paperwork when I get back. But the transfer may take a while."

"I understand," Father said.

Peter jumped up as soon as Mr. Ranta had closed the door. "Orchestra hall, here I come," he said.

Once Peter knew they were moving to Petrozavodsk, he decided to learn Russian. "You and Maija will be going to a Finnish school, Hub," Peter said, "but if I want to audition for the orchestra and get into college, I'll need to know Russian." Peter borrowed some books from an Uhtua teacher, and once a week he skied to the village for tutoring. When Peter practiced his lessons at home, Father shook his head. "I hope everyone talks Finn at the ski factory," he said. "That Russian sounds like someone's spitting nails."

PART II
THE RED
BROOM SWEEPS
JUNE 1935
LÖNNROT TO PETROZAVODSK

SWAMP STREET

On June tenth, Karlov finally brought the news that Father had been assigned to the Gylling Ski Factory in Petrozavodsk.

"You shouldn't have any trouble managing the mill," Father said to Karlov as they prepared to leave Lönnrot.

"That is true," Karlov replied.

Jake was angry at the stiff-lipped Russian. Couldn't he at least thank Father for all his work? Without Father's advice, Karlov would have set up the sawmill in a mud hole.

"Just make sure that you keep the equipment well oiled," Father said. "No sense being penny wise and pound foolish."

"I will monitor the lubrication myself," Karlov said. Though Medved paused to give Maija's hand a friendly lick, Karlov walked away without even saying good-bye.

When the Makis arrived in Petrozavodsk, Jake was disappointed. The train depot was a low, dirty building with chipped gray paint. Compared to the fancy dome and brass clock of Grand Central Station in New York, it was a dump.

A group of soldiers who had gotten out of the train car ahead of them marched up the street. Their uniforms were torn in several places, and one man's toe stuck out of his boot.

"What's that smell?" Maija said.

"It must be cabbage," Mother said.

"No, the other smell."

"It's coming from there." Jake pointed to a rattly horse-drawn wagon that was pulling a wooden tank down the street. Something was leaving a dark trail on the dusty cobblestones. "It stinks like sewage."

"Surely not." Mother wrinkled up her nose.

"I am afraid your son is correct." It was the conductor from the Kem train. "We call that the honey wagon. Sanitation is not all it should be."

"Dear me." Mother stared after the wagon.

"In any case," the conductor turned to reboard the train, "welcome to Petrozavodsk."

"Isn't this the capital city?" Mother said.

"It has twenty thousand people," Father said.

"But the streets aren't even paved," Jake said.

"If the need is great, then so is the potential," Father said.

Jake had expected Petrozavodsk to be a commercial center like the big towns on the Mesabi Range. But it looked more like a country village. A herd of goats wandered past the station. The unpainted log shacks had grimy windows and yards that were crowded with vegetable gardens, chicken coops, and pigpens. The dirt side streets were rutted from the wheels of horse-drawn wagons. The few cars were rusty old junkers. Chimney smoke clouded the skyline.

"I wonder where Ranta could be." Father pulled out his watch. "I'm going to check inside the station."

"We'll come, too," Mother said as she and Maija followed.

"Let's find a bathroom," Jake said.

"Who knows how long we'll be standing here." Peter agreed.

When the boys returned, Peter stopped suddenly. "My clarinet!"

"It must be somewhere." Jake helped him unpile their packs. "Maybe Mother put it in her trunk?"

"It's gone." Peter shook his head and pointed to an empty spot on the stained wooden platform. "I left it right there."

Just then, Mother and Father returned. "Is something wrong?" Mother asked.

"Someone's stolen my clarinet."

"No!" Mother cried.

"Why weren't you watching?" Father glared at Jake.

"It's not his fault," Peter said. "We left for a minute."

Father's eyes stayed on Jake. "Were you wasting time playing with that baseball?"

"Father." Peter took him by the arm. "It was my clarinet. I should have kept an eye on it."

At that moment, Mr. Ranta appeared. "Excuse me for being late" — he took off his cap — "but the train is so seldom on time." He looked at Mother and Maija. "Is there a problem?"

"My son's clarinet has been stolen!" Mother nearly shouted.

"I am sorry, Mrs. Maki." Ranta stayed calm. "Unfortunately, petty thievery has been a problem of late."

"But Peter needs his instrument."

"All we can do is report this matter to the authorities."

He shook Father's hand. "I'm glad that you could come, Arvid. I am certain you will contribute much to our enterprise."

Mr. Ranta helped the family load their things into his old Ford truck. "If the children won't mind riding in the back, I will show you the ski factory before I take you to your barracks."

As Jake climbed into the back of the pickup he told Peter, "I can't believe you're not more upset. If someone had stolen my baseball glove, I'd be crazy."

"It's only a clarinet, Hub," Peter said.

"But what about your practicing?"

"If I can't find another instrument, I'll study music theory. It's almost more fun to imagine the notes in my head."

The transmission clanked as Ranta shifted the truck into gear and raced the smoky engine.

"It sounds like it's ready to explode," Maija said.

"Hang on," Peter said, reaching out to keep Maija from tipping over as the truck jerked forward.

Mr. Ranta parked his truck in front of the Gylling Ski Factory and everyone climbed out. The plant was larger than Jake had expected. Surrounded by high wire fences and guard dogs tethered to wire ropes, the buildings extended along the shore of Lake Onega.

"As you can see, we have an extensive operation. This is the second largest factory in Petrozavodsk. We employ 250 workers." Ranta nodded to a guard at the main gate. "Over there is the powerhouse — it's fueled by our own wood scraps — and beyond that is the lumberyard. We also have a woodworking shop and a machine shop. I could take you inside, but I imagine you would like to get settled in your new home."

"That would be nice." Mother sighed.

As they walked back toward the truck, a black car rounded the corner at high speed and threw up a plume of dust before it sped out of sight. It was Ed Salo's black Buick!

Jake turned to see if Father had noticed. He was staring, too. "Whose car was that?" Father asked.

"Isn't it a dandy? The head of the NKVD drives that car. It's his pride and joy."

"The NKVD?"

"The secret police."

Jake's mouth dropped open. The secret police! So much for Salo's gift to the people. Jake was waiting for Father to say something more, but he only frowned.

A few moments later, Mr. Ranta parked in front of the barracks, a half dozen two-story log apartments just up the street from the ski factory. As they jumped out of the truck, a line of soldiers marched past. "There's more soldiers than people in this town," Maija said.

Ranta smiled. "It may seem that way at times." Then he led them up a short flight of stairs and through a doorway. "I was hoping a larger apartment would be available," he said, "but until one opens up, you'll have to make do."

"Won't it be fine to have a room all to ourselves?" Father spoke as he held the door open. Mother tried to smile, but Jake could tell she was still numb from Peter's loss.

Ranta showed them to a small room at the end of the hall. "I'm afraid this was originally designed as a toilet."

Mother studied the unpainted room.

"But, of course, no one has ever used it for that," Mr. Ranta said. "When the Canadians and Americans arrived, they decided it was more sensible to build the outhouses in back. Now there's one outdoor toilet for each group of four families."

As Mr. Ranta was getting ready to leave, Mother asked, "And what will our address be?"

"Sixty-six *Bolotnaya Ulitsa*," Ranta said.

"What does *Bolotnaya Ulitsa* translate to?" Father asked.

"Swamp Street." Ranta smiled, tipping his cap as he left.

LIFE IN THE TOILET

I can't believe they've put us in a toilet on Swamp Street," Jake said, dropping his pack to the floor.

"Don't say that," Father said. "You heard Ranta explain that it was only called a toilet in the original building design."

"But it's so small, Arvid," Mother said.

"This will be an improvement over hiding behind sheets like we did at Lönnrot," Father said.

"I suppose." Mother sounded unconvinced.

Peter paced off the size of the room. "Twelve feet by fifteen," he said. "In square footage that comes to —"

"Spare us the details," Father said.

"This whole apartment is smaller than our living room back in Finntown," Maija said, squinting in the light that streamed through the single filmy window.

"Enough complaining," Father said.

"It doesn't look like our bed will fit." Mother frowned.

"Karlov said that he'd wait until we ask to have it sent," Father said. "I'm sure we'll find a larger place soon."

Two sets of bunk beds and a folding cot were crammed into one end of the room. The opposite side held a wood cookstove and a rust-stained sink. Jake had hoped they would have indoor plumbing in the city, but the slop bucket under the sink told a different story.

"We've even got our own dining room furniture," Father said, pointing at the square table and tippy benches that looked like they had been hammered together out of wood scraps.

Jake saw tears well up in Mother's eyes. He wondered if she was thinking of the sturdy oak table they'd auctioned off before they left Minnesota.

Despite the cramped conditions in their apartment, the Makis discovered advantages to life in Petrozavodsk. Mother met two friendly ladies named Hanna Seppi and Edith Kesänen, who lived in the barracks. Edith's daughter,

Lempi, was the same age as Maija, and Hanna's baby, William, was a favorite with everyone. Even Father liked to bounce little William on his knee and tickle him.

The first time Jake walked behind the barracks, he met a boy named Aarne Jokinen, who was throwing a rubber ball against the fence and catching it barehanded. Aarne was a pale boy with brown hair and deep-set eyes.

"You've got a glove!" Aarne said.

"My brother has one, too. I'll bet he'd let you borrow it."

"Really?" Aarne's eyes lit up. "My friends and I have been playing baseball for a couple years, but only two fellows have gloves."

"I didn't think anyone played ball in Russia," Jake said.

"A man named Red Lonn moved here from Detroit and brought over a bunch of equipment. But the older guys got all the good stuff. Red's even got a baseball autographed by Babe Ruth!"

"How many guys play in the neighborhood?" Jake asked.

"Nine or ten. Not enough for a real game."

"Don't you ever play Rotation?" Jake asked.

When Aarne shook his head, Jake got excited. "How soon can you get the guys together?"

By the end of the day, Jake had showed Aarne and his

friends Rotation, a game that gave everyone a chance at each position. Though half the boys spoke Finnish and half Russian, and though they only had two bats and four gloves to share between them, everyone had a great time.

The next day, Aarne showed Jake a good fishing spot near some pilings north of the ski factory. They only caught perch, but it reminded Jake of fishing off the Silver Lake trestle back home. As the boys dangled their lines, Jake asked, "How long have you lived in Petrozavodsk?"

"We moved here from Suomussalmi, Finland, when I was eight years old. My father got a job as a truck driver."

"You speak Finnish like Victor Karlov."

"Who's that?"

"A man I hope to never see again."

"You'd sound Russian, too, if you'd gone to school here since second grade."

When Jake brought home a pail full of fish, Father said, "Now that's what I call making good use of your time. Not like that baseball."

From the start, Father found Petrozavodsk to his liking. The city had a community of Finnish immigrants who shared Father's dream of building a workers' paradise. Father's favorite place was a Finnish bookstore, where he enjoyed sharing his political views with the other customers.

He met a man at the store named Oscar Corgan, who had been director of the Karelian Technical Aid in New York. Mr. Corgan now worked for the Kirja Publishing House on the second floor of the bookstore building. He and Father often discussed socialist principles.

In addition to working five days a week at the ski factory, Father also volunteered his Saturdays to the *Subbotniks*, volunteer public works crews that built sidewalks, parks, and other city improvements. Finns and Russians worked side by side on the biggest project, constructing wooden pipes to bring water from Lake Onega to the city. "Just think how nice it will be to have running water," Father said.

"Don't we have running water already?" Peter asked.

When Mother and Father both frowned, Peter laughed and said, "Isn't Jake always running to get it?"

Mother was impressed with the city's cultural events. In addition to Finnish radio and theater productions, there were poetry recitations, debate and declamation events, and Petrozavodsk's famous orchestra. Jake was excited to find clubs for track, gymnastics, skiing, wrestling, and target shooting.

But the thing that Mother appreciated most was the

special immigrant store. She found out about it when Edith and Hanna asked, "Have you been to the INSNAB?"

"The what?"

"The INSNAB," Hanna said. "That's short for *Inostrannyyoje snabzheniye*. It's a shop reserved for immigrants. You can buy things the Russian stores rarely stock, like butter and meat and oil."

"How do I find this place?"

"It's nearby," Edith said. "All you need is a ration card. I'll take you to the government office and help you register."

Mother was also excited to find that an immigrant incentive boosted Father's wages thirty percent. "Didn't I tell you the Party would look out for its own?" Father said.

Father brought more good news home after his first month at the factory. "I've been promoted," he said.

"Already?" Mother said.

"They've transferred me to the wood shop." Father smiled. "I'll be working under Ranta and an engineer named Snellman."

"We're so proud of you, Father." Maija gave him a hug.

He kissed her cheek. "And I have another surprise," he said, stepping into the hallway. He set a long gray case on the table.

"A clarinet!" Peter opened the lid.

"Ranta knows someone in the orchestra."

"Surely we can't afford an instrument this fine," Peter said, fingering the brightly polished keys.

"You used the fifty dollars from Urho, didn't you?" Mother said. "That was supposed to be our emergency fund."

"With all the hours that Peter has practiced, he deserves the best."

Jake hadn't seen Father this excited since the night Mother had agreed to move to Karelia. "And Jaakko . . ."

"Yes?" Jake said, worried that he'd done something wrong.

"I've got news for you, too. Since we're going to need fellows to test skis, I volunteered your services."

"You mean I'd get to try brand-new skis?" Jake said.

"We'll be fitting you as soon as it snows," Father said. "And it just may pay a little, too."

"They'd give me money to ski?"

"At least pocket change."

"But your schooling will have to come first," Mother said.

INSNAB

The following afternoon, Jake was finishing up a letter to Joe, telling him about his new friends, when Mother asked, "Would you help me carry some groceries home from the INSNAB store?"

Jake hated shopping, but he couldn't refuse, since Peter was practicing his clarinet and Maija was playing with Edith Kesänen's daughter, Lempi.

On their way to the store, they walked past the honey-wagon driver, who was parked on a side street and having lunch. Mother looked away as the dark-bearded man chewed off a hunk of black bread and washed it down with a swig of vodka.

When they reached the INSNAB, Jake was disappointed to find most of the shelves bare. He expected the store would be like the Co-op Store back home. But if this was the best-equipped market in the city, he couldn't imagine how empty the Russian stores must be.

Later that afternoon, Jake asked Aarne if his mother shopped at the INSNAB, and Aarne said, "She can't."

"I thought it was for immigrants."

"We're border hoppers without official papers. There's lots more of us in town than you legal immigrants."

"That's unfair," Jake said.

"My mom's used to standing in line at the Russian store."

"A recruiter told us there was bread for all in Russia."

"There is." Aarne smiled. "But sometimes you have to wait a long time to get it."

A few days after Peter got his new clarinet, he asked Jake to help him find the orchestra hall. Following Hanna Seppi's directions, they walked up the hill after breakfast. "Isn't this a little early for a concert?" Jake asked.

"I heard the orchestra practices in the morning."

When they arrived at the square that Mrs. Seppi had described, Peter said, "It should be near here."

"I'll bet it's right over there." Jake pointed.

98

"How can you be so sure?"

"Just listen."

Peter grinned when he heard the clear chords of the violins and cellos. They hurried down the block until they reached the open door of the Philharmonic Hall. The boys stepped inside. Music filled the whole lobby. Peter whispered, "Can you believe the acoustics? No wonder musicians travel from all over the country to play here."

Jake and Peter slipped into the shadows by the back wall. The men and women onstage wore ordinary clothes, yet they were playing an extraordinarily beautiful composition. Unlike the decorative Socialist Opera Hall in Finntown, the interior of this high-ceilinged auditorium was simple and severe.

"No! No! No!" A shout interrupted Jake's thoughts. For a moment, he feared someone was yelling at them for sneaking in. Then the conductor rapped his baton on the podium and bellowed, "*Fortissimo!* How many times must I tell you? *Fortissimo!*"

Jake and Peter crept back outside. "That fellow outyelled the whole orchestra," Jake said. "What were they doing wrong?"

Peter looked worried. "It sounded perfect to me," he said. "I'd better get home and practice."

Without knowing it, Father put even more pressure on Peter when he said, "Getting into that little band should be a breeze for a man with your talent."

"It may not be that easy, Father," Peter said. "The orchestra is mainly adults, and they've played for many years."

"The folks back home nicknamed you Genius for good reason," Father said. "I know you can do it."

THE GRAY HOUSE

Although Aarne couldn't understand why a Rogers Hornsby baseball card was more valuable than a Benny Bengough, he enjoyed looking through Jake's collection. Even after Jake taught Aarne about ABs, hits, runs, RBIs, SOs, and batting averages, Aarne still picked Napoleon Lajoie as his favorite player.

Late one afternoon, Aarne showed Jake a park that lay between Volodarsky and Uritsky streets. "Wait till you see this," he said. He led Jake to an overgrown area beside the path and parted some hawthorn branches.

A statue was tipped over in the brush. "It's huge!" Jake

said, studying the bronze face that was half covered with leaf litter. "Who is it?"

"Peter the Great. Some folks joke that he's been deposed."

"More like disposed." Jake studied the kind profile of the giant and the massive arm that was extended in a gesture of friendship. "I thought Peter was a hero to the Russians."

"Times change," Aarne said.

The most beautiful, and at the same time, the saddest place in the city to Jake was Petrozavodsk Cathedral. Jake drew several sketches of the vacant church that was falling into ruin. Whenever he looked at the five golden cross-topped domes and the arched entrances, he imagined the work it must have taken to cut and fit those ancient stones. Two smoke-scorched foundations nearby showed that smaller churches had been burned in recent times.

"The first year we moved to Petrozavodsk, the bells still rang from the cathedral tower," Aarne said. "On a quiet morning, the tolling echoed all through the town and out over the lake."

"What happened?" Jake asked.

"They passed a law that banned ringing the bells. Then

the government ordered the bells melted down for weapon making."

"I know socialists don't believe in churchgoing, but it's a crime not to preserve such a beautiful building."

"Be careful of what you say," Aarne warned.

"Why should I?" Jake was shocked at Aarne's tone. His voice suddenly sounded cold and stiff like Victor Karlov's.

"It isn't wise to question a decision of the government."

"My father says that debate is healthy," Jake said.

"Some people would consider your father a dangerous man," Aarne said. "Let me show you something."

Aarne led Jake to a forbidding four-story brick building on Komsomolskaya Street. Jake asked, "Why are the windows barred?"

Before Aarne spoke he looked to see if anyone was watching. "They call it the Gray House."

"Is it a prison?" Jake stopped to get a better look.

"Keep walking."

"Can't we go closer?"

"We shouldn't be this close."

Just then, a black car wheeled around the corner and pulled up in front of the Gray House. It was Salo's Buick again! The driver opened the back door, and a man in a black hat and coat strode toward the building with a body-guard on each side.

"That's Ed Salo's car," Jake said. "He donated it to the Party, but somehow that man has stolen it."

"Stop staring!" Aarne walked faster. "And I wouldn't repeat such lies."

"But I'm telling the truth."

"Some things are best left unspoken."

Jake was puzzled until they reached the end of the block and Aarne explained. "That was the NKVD headquarters."

"The secret police?" Jake asked.

Aarne nodded. "They can arrest anyone at any time."

"Without a warrant?"

"And imprison them without a trial," Aarne said. "My father says there are two more stories of the Gray House belowground. Those rooms are for questioning prisoners."

When Jake looked doubtful, Aarne said, "It's true. The neighbors have all heard screams in the middle of the night."

"Why isn't there an investigation?" Jake said.

"How can you investigate if the men who are taken into that building never come out again?"

When Father got home from work, Jake told him about the Gray House, but he only said, "Don't waste your energy on gossip." Then he turned to the family.

"I've got more news from the factory. They've given me the Stakhanovite award."

"Is that good?" Maija asked.

"Yes." Father laughed. "It's a Russian word that means I've been exceeding my daily quotas."

"Congratulations," Mother said.

When Peter finally got the courage to audition for the orchestra, he received disappointing news. "The conductor said that my ear was excellent," Peter explained, "but my technique needed seasoning."

"Seasoning?" Father said. "What kind of talk is that? Does he think you are some kind of vegetable?"

"He's a very smart man."

"I have a mind to write him a letter."

"No, Father. He says I'll improve fast if I practice with the *Penikka Panti*."

"The Puppy Band?"

"They only call it that because the members are young."

"It sounds like a waste of your talent," Father said.

"I'll do whatever it takes," Peter said.

"All right, then. But tell those puppy players to come up with a better name for themselves."

FINN OR FINGLISH?

In the fall, Jake and Maija enrolled in the Finnish school. Since Mother had continued to tutor Jake through the summer, he was confident he would do well.

However, he got a surprise on the first day. His Finnish teacher was a short lady with a stern voice named Mrs. Sippola. After she called the roll, she looked at the class over the top of her glasses and asked, "How many of you speak Finnish?"

Jake raised his hand along with everyone else. Their faces said, Of course we speak Finnish, we're Finns, aren't we?

"Very well," Mrs. Sippola said. "I will test you with a

few simple words." She held up a picture of a telephone and asked a girl in the front row. "What is this?"

"A *telefooni*," the girl replied.

"How many of you agree?"

Nearly everyone raised their hands.

"I'm sorry to say that you are wrong. This is a *puhelin*."

The class wondered if this teacher was playing a trick on them. Next she turned to Jake and asked, "What do you get when you go to the barber?"

This was easy, Jake thought. He said, "A *heerkatti*," and the class nodded in agreement.

"Wrong again," she said. "You get a *tukanleikkuu*."

Mrs. Sippola went on to ask students to identify a dozen more words, and they missed every single one.

How can everyone be wrong at the same time? Jake wondered. Was this kind-faced teacher meaner than she looked?

After giving the class a moment to think, she asked, "Can anyone explain why none of you, who appear to be very smart young people, know such basic Finnish words?"

When no one raised their hand, she said, "I can't blame you for not knowing the answer. The fact is, you don't speak real Finnish. You speak an American form of Finnish — some people call it Finglish."

The class laughed when she said "Finglish," but she had made her point.

Then Mrs. Sippola smiled and repeated her first question: "So how many of you think you speak Finnish now?"

This time only one boy in the back corner raised his hand.

"Are you from the U.S. or Canada?" she asked.

"I'm from Helsinki," he said.

"I was hoping that we would have one real Finn in our class," she said. "You will be my teaching assistant."

Peter learned about something even stranger than Finglish in his college classes. Through the summer, he'd improved his Russian enough to be admitted to the university. Peter admired his music, mathematics, and science instructors, but Jake asked him why he never said anything about his other teachers.

Peter frowned. "I'm still trying to figure them out."

"Why is that?"

"My regular classes are going fine, but I have one course called the History of the Communist Party of the Soviet Union that's one hundred percent Marxism. There are so many great thinkers in the world, but we only study Karl Marx. The other morning I joked with my friends that if Karl joined up with Groucho, Chico, and Harpo, he could be the fourth Marx Brother. They stared at me like I'd broken some law. But the class that bothers me most is called War Studies. The teacher says we need to make ourselves ready for the final conflict with the capitalist exploiters. A big part of the class is rifle range practice."

"By final conflict does he mean war?" Jake asked.

"And you can guess who the capitalist exploiters are."

"They're preparing to fight America?" Jake was stunned.

"I'm afraid so, Hub."

Jake suddenly understood his brother's worries. Building a socialist society was one thing, but planning to wage war on America was a possibility that he'd never considered.

REVOLUTION DAY

Jake was surprised to find that the Russians held an event similar to America's Fourth of July on November 7. Called October Revolution Day, it honored Lenin's rise to power in 1917. To prepare for the big parade, city workers built a review stand and strung up a huge banner:

LONG LIVE THE GREAT AND INVINCIBLE PARTY OF

MARX — ENGELS — LENIN — STALIN!

Several Party officials traveled all the way from Moscow to participate. The head of the delegation gave a speech praising the citizens of Petrozavodsk, and he singled out the men at the ski factory, calling them "models of Soviet efficiency."

Jake watched Father and his friends raise their heads high. The man concluded by urging everyone to give their eternal thanks to the leader of the Communist Party, Joseph Stalin, "the lighter of the sun, and the giver of all gifts."

On the way home, Peter asked Father, "I thought you said that Edvard Gylling would be giving a speech today."

"Everyone from the factory hoped that he would appear. I assume he was called away on official business."

"Edith Kesänen heard a rumor that Gylling has been arrested," Mother said.

"That's ridiculous," Father said. "There isn't a man more loyal to the Party or more humble. With a title like Chairman of the Council of People's Commissars, he could have been arrogant, but he visited our workstations like he was one of us. His replacement is a wretched little bureaucrat who is afraid to set foot in the factory without a crew of armed bodyguards beside him."

"I fear the worst may have happened," Mother said.

"Don't say that. Now that Kirov and Roivo are gone, Gylling is our last, best hope."

■   ■   ■

Only a few days later, Father came home angry. "Where's my letter-writing paper, Annikki?"

"Are you going to ask for a transfer back to Lönnrot?" Mother teased. "I thought you liked your work here."

"How can they call this an election day when they put only one name on the ballot?"

"Surely you're not writing to Moscow about that?"

"I should address this to Joseph Stalin himself," Father said. "Voters deserve a healthy airing of ideas. Do they expect a politician to debate with himself?"

"I don't know if it's wise to complain so publicly, Arvid," Mother said. "Can't you just speak with someone?"

"A man has a duty to fight injustice." Father took up his pen. "Open discussion is the heart of a strong society."

Later that same week, Father found out that the stories of Edvard Gylling's arrest were true.

"But why would they ever arrest him?" Jake asked.

"There's no telling," Father said. "They say that the Party is purging itself of all who are disloyal."

"But you've always said Gylling was dedicated," Peter said.

"I know they wouldn't arrest an innocent man."

"Won't the lighter of the sun protect him?" Maija asked.

"What sort of nonsense is that?" Father said.

"Didn't the man from Moscow call Mr. Stalin the lighter of the sun? If Stalin is so powerful, can't he help Gylling?"

Father opened his mouth, then he stopped. "We may not know the whole story."

"That's what I'm afraid of," Mother said. "First Kirov is killed. Now Gylling disappears. Who do you suppose is next?"

Only a few days later, Father came home and said, "Aaro Holopainen has been convicted of sabotage."

"Isn't he only a dairy farmer?" Mother asked.

Father nodded. "He managed a big farm outside town. One of his milkmaids accidentally poisoned the herd, and 150 cows died. Yet he was still sentenced to three years in jail."

"How can they call an accident sabotage?" Jake asked.

Father hesitated, then he said, "There must be a reason."

"I think his real crime was being a Finn," Jake said.

An event that saddened Jake even more happened on a cool autumn night. Jake was jarred out of his sleep by a far-off rumbling. He sat up and whispered to Peter, "Was it thunder?"

"It's too late in the fall," Peter said.

Jake tiptoed to the window and looked out. The night was clear and still. After Jake lay back down, he listened for a long time, but it remained quiet.

The next morning, Jake and Aarne were walking to school, when Jake looked up and said, "The cathedral is gone."

"You're crazy," Aarne said.

"Where is it, then?" Both boys searched the skyline, but the familiar domed steeples were gone.

"Let's see what happened," Jake said. They ran to the site of the old church. Two dozen soldiers were guarding a pile of rubble. "They blew the whole thing up!"

"Not so loud," Aarne warned.

Jake stared at the crumbled stones. A fine dust floated in the sunlight, along with a strong powder smell. "I can understand melting cathedral bells to make weapons," Jake said. "But why destroy such a beautiful old building?"

"Hush up," Aarne said, "or they'll hear you."

Jake felt like shouting. Seeing the senseless damage left an empty feeling inside him.

As the days went on, workmen labored to haul away the broken stones, but Jake still couldn't walk past the ruin without feeling an anger, and at the same time, a chill.

. . .

Winter came early to Petrozavodsk. In November, Jake had to shovel nearly every day. The snow-packed streets became so slippery that it was difficult to get around the city. One evening after Jake helped Mother carry home a sack of flour, he had an idea. "Do you remember the kick sled that Uncle Urho had out at his farm?" he asked Father.

"The *Potkukelkka*? Of course."

"Wouldn't a kick sled be perfect for hauling in the city?"

"Perhaps," Father said.

"Why doesn't the ski factory build some?"

"I just may suggest that to Ranta," Father said.

Two weeks later, Father took Jake aside on a Saturday morning. "If you're caught up with your chores, would you like to come to the factory with me?"

"The wood box and water buckets are full," Mother said.

"Good," Father said. "I've picked out a new model of skis that should be a perfect fit."

"Do I get to test them?"

Father nodded. "We've been experimenting with a longer glide zone, and I'd like to see how fast they are."

When they got to the factory, Father showed Jake the skis. Then he took him to another room. "And look what we have here."

"A kick sled!" Jake said. Father had built a Finnish sled with steel runners, steering handles, and a rider's chair.

"Thanks to your idea," Father said. "It's only a prototype, but Ranta hopes to have it in production soon."

Only a few minutes later, Jake was racing up the Lososinka River through a fresh dusting of snow. As Father had promised, the new skis were lighter and faster than the ones they'd made last winter. Jake sped out of the city and into a forest of birch and pine.

He quickly fell into the familiar rhythm of kick, pole, and glide. Jake had forgotten how free it felt to ski. Squirrels and birds chattered in the background as he crouched on the downhill slopes and his skis hissed beneath him.

Though the new skis were fast, they tended to slip when he poled uphill. And after Jake returned to the factory, the designers listened carefully to his comments. They even recorded his height and weight on a chart next to the name of the skis that he had tried.

"I didn't know it was that scientific," Jake said.

Father showed Jake a second chart. "We also keep track of the temperature, snow conditions, and wax formula."

Once Jake settled into the routine of the Finnish school, he enjoyed it more than he thought he would. His teachers were dedicated to promoting Finnish culture, and like Father, they were anxious to build an independent Finnish state in Russia. Everyone hoped that if enough Finns migrated to Karelia, they could replace the Russians as the dominant political group.

Whether Jake was studying science or mathematics or geography, his teachers tied their lessons to Finnish culture and history. He learned about the foreign powers that had controlled Finland, the revolutions it had survived, and the great literature, music, and art it had produced. Jake's physical education teacher taught him about famous Finnish Olympic champions such as Paavo Nurmi, Hannes Kolehmainen, Veli Saarinen, and Anton Collin.

But Jake's favorite teacher was Mrs. Sippola. She made her lessons fun, and she had a clever way of turning mistakes into jokes that the students could learn from. Once each week, she brought in an English or American poem and asked the class to translate it into Finnish. Sometimes it was Whitman, other times Shakespeare or Byron. One day she picked "Stopping by Woods on a Snowy Evening" by Robert Frost. Jake had studied the poem before, but Mrs. Sippola explained it much more clearly. She introduced the poem on December twentieth and asked, "Why do you suppose I chose this poem for today?"

Jake read through the poem and raised his hand. "Is it the phrase, 'The darkest evening of the year'?"

"Very good, Jaakko. Why do you say that?"

"In science we learned that the winter solstice, the shortest day of the year, is happening tomorrow."

"Indeed it is," Mrs. Sippola said. "And that will most certainly help us understand Frost's message."

THE RITES OF WINTER

When the Makis celebrated their second Christmas in Karelia, Father surprised everyone by buying a used crystal radio from a coworker. He brought it home on Christmas Eve. "I know I should have waited until Father Frost's Day, but I think the socialists will forgive us," he said.

Jake responded by giving Father and Mother a present of his own. He'd traded a pile of his baseball cards for a small package of coffee. "Jaakko!" Father said when Mother opened the sack. "This is our best present ever."

So while Peter tuned in the Petrozavodsk Radio Symphony Orchestra, Mother started the coffee boiling.

The warm fire and the smell of fresh coffee rising from the stove almost made it seem like a real Christmas celebration after all.

From that evening on, the family never missed an orchestra broadcast. For practice, Peter played along, impressing Jake by how he could pick out the notes of a song after hearing it only once. And Mother, who rarely sang anymore, sometimes hummed to herself as she knitted in front of the stove.

Jake had written to Joe three times since they'd moved to the city, but he didn't receive a reply until two days after Christmas. Joe's letter looked like it had spent a long time in the government censor's office. Several long passages that probably contained news had been blacked out, but the sports was untouched.

> The World Series was a real bust, Jake. That bunch of dummies from St. Louis they call the "Gashouse Gang" — Paul and Dizzy Dean, Leo Durocher, Joe Medwick, and Pepper Martin — whooped the Tigers real bad. I know you can't stand that Mister Big Britches, Dizzy Dean, but he was unhittable. These days it's hard to argue with Dizzy's famous saying: "It ain't bragging if you can do it."

Since Joe didn't mention the letters Jake had sent him, he guessed they'd been intercepted by the censors. Jake hadn't written about politics, so he couldn't understand why anyone would bother to stop his mail.

At first, Jake found his winter chores simpler in Petrozavodsk than they had been at Lönnrot. It was easier to winch the water bucket out of the well than it had been to chop a hole in the lake. But once the north winds began to blow, it got so cold that Jake had to throw the bucket down the well several times each morning to break the ice. And some days Jake had to lean into the well and crack the surface with an iron pipe.

Soon the top of the well was covered with ice. Father and Peter helped Jake chop it free, but in a few days, it mounded over again. Jake discovered that if he laid boards and hay over the well only a thin layer of ice formed. The other folks in the neighborhood copied him, and Father complimented him, saying, "You should be called the Stakhanovite of the barracks for such an idea."

The hardest winter job of all was washing clothes. Each Saturday morning, Jake and Maija helped Mother fill the boiler on top of the woodstove. After the water warmed, they filled a metal tub and scrubbed the clothes on a washboard. Then they loaded the clothes on a sled and pulled it down to the Lososinka River, where they rinsed the clothes in the current by swishing them with a long stick. Once they returned home, the frozen clothing had to be thawed with warm water and run through a wringer before they could hang them outside to freeze dry.

Jake's ski testing became even more fun when Mr. Ranta invited Aarne to help Jake. Together they plotted a course along the Lososinka and back through the woods. Though Jake had longer legs than Aarne, their races were close. The loser always blamed the equipment, saying, "You must have the faster skis today."

Jake and Aarne entered several ski competitions during the winter. Father and his friends from the factory always cheered them on. In one event, Jake won first prize, a .22-caliber rifle. Father made a shoulder sling so Jake could take the rifle with him when he skied. The rabbits and squirrels that Jake brought home were a welcome addition to Mother's stew pot. Jake even shot two black grouse that were twice as big as the partridge back in Minnesota.

■   ■   ■

By midwinter, the ski factory's kick sleds had become commonplace in the city. People used them for hauling groceries and firewood and even commuting to work. The hard-packed snow became known as *pääkallo keli,* or "skull condition," because reckless drivers often cracked their heads when they spilled.

One night in February, Father said, "With my new production bonus — and we have Jake's sled idea to thank for that — I've been drawing up some plans. I didn't want to get your hopes up in case it wasn't approved, but —"

"If what wasn't approved?" Mother said.

"Four of us fellows from the U.S. have permission to build an apartment house."

"For whom?" Mother asked.

"For us," Father said. "Oscar Corgan gave me the idea — he's working on one, too."

"But what about the money?"

"The government is helping with the financing. We'll have two bedrooms and a kitchen with built-in cupboards. We can finally ask Karlov to send down our bed."

"Oh, Arvid." Mother smiled. "That's the best news ever."

"There'll be a community sauna, and as more fellows sign up, we'll be putting up an athletic field for the young people."

"As long as we're sharing good news," Peter said. "The conductor of the Petrozavodsk Orchestra sat in on our school concert this afternoon, and he invited me to try out again."

"My son is graduating from the Puppy Band!" Father said.

"That's wonderful," Mother said, giving Peter a big hug.

Spring found Father so involved in his plans for a new home that he didn't notice how the attitude toward Finnish Americans had begun to change. One day when Aarne and Jake were coming home from playing baseball, Aarne told Jake that he'd overheard a Russian soldier talking about getting even with the capitalist Americans who were playacting at socialism.

"My father is as dedicated as any Russian," Jake said.

"I know," Aarne said, "but even our friends who have come here from Finland are upset at how some of the Americans flash their money and flaunt their fur coats and jewelry."

"My mother has had the same old coat for ten years."

"I just wanted to warn you," Aarne said.

Yet Father remained positive. He worked five days at the ski factory and volunteered his Saturdays to the *Subbotnik* labor crew. If that wasn't enough, he spent all day Sunday and most evenings working on the apartment house.

Father was so tired that he could barely lift himself out of bed, yet his faith in socialism remained strong. When his application for membership in the Soviet Communist Party was finally approved, he said, "Russia has accepted us at last."

Jake had almost forgotten about Aarne's warning, when he came home one day to find Mother crying. "What's wrong?" he asked.

"The INSNAB closed this morning." She dabbed her eyes. "I stood in line all morning long at the Russian store for that —" She pointed to a single loaf of rye.

When Father got home from work, he refused to get upset. "We'll just have to eat like the Russians from now on, Annikki," he said. "I was uneasy about those special privileges anyway."

From then on, Mother had to line up at five in the morning when she needed to buy bread.

Father even remained patient when the government financing was canceled on his half-completed apartment building. "We'll finish it as soon as the economy turns around," he promised.

The only time Jake saw Father disturbed was when the

Supreme Soviet changed the ski factory to a six-day week. "They said the motherland would be able to build lots more fighter planes and battleships if us workers put in extra hours," Father said, "and not one soul spoke up."

"You didn't say anything, did you, Arvid?" Mother asked.

"I would have held my tongue, but on top of the increase in hours, they plan to fine a person every time they're late for work and put them in jail after a third tardiness."

"That does sound extreme," Mother said.

"I raised my hand and asked, 'How can you punish fellows for being late when there isn't an alarm clock for sale in the city?'"

"What did they say?"

"They're forwarding my suggestion to some committee."

"I'll bet your suggestion will end up in the same office as those letters that you wrote from the lumber camp," Jake said.

Father laughed. "I don't doubt it."

"I wish you'd be more careful, Arvid," Mother said.

"Somebody's got to keep those bureaucrats busy."

IN THE VALLEY OF THE SHADOW

Despite having to work an extra day at the factory during all of 1936, Father remained enthusiastic. "Now that Russia is our home, we must do our best to help the socialist cause," he said.

But Petrozavodsk was feeling less like home to Jake. As the fall of 1937 approached, the NKVD took several of the Makis' neighbors in for questioning. None returned. When Mother told Father she was worried, he only said, "We have the protection of Party membership now. They will look out for us."

Even when one of his friends at the factory, Emil Soderstrom, was arrested, Father said, "Emil had a record in Finland. It's likely he got into something illegal over here."

"Wouldn't it be safer to go back to the U.S.?" Jake asked more times than he could count. But Father wouldn't listen. It made no difference that his friend Joe reported that the economy was improving back home. For once Joe's letter had slipped through the censors unmarked. *President Roosevelt's new programs are putting lots of people back to work*, Joe wrote. But his main interest was the All-Star Game. Jake figured Joe had only mentioned Roosevelt because he was there to throw out the first pitch. *The big news is Dizzy Dean got his toe broken by a line drive in the third inning*, Joe wrote. *Hooray for Earl Averill! He gave that blowhard what he deserved*. Though Jake agreed that Dizzy was stuck on himself, he wrote back and said it wasn't right to celebrate a fellow getting hurt.

For the first time in his life, Jake wasn't thinking about baseball. Like everyone else, he was worried about the NKVD, who were arresting more people all the time. Jake and Aarne often heard the secret police knocking on their neighbors' doors in the middle of the night. And nearly every morning men were being arrested at their workplaces.

Jake heard that a kindly actor named Otto Bjorinen was taken. Then Väino Finberg, a loyal Party member, disappeared without warning, along with good citizens such as Olavi Siikki and Kalle Sevander. In each case, the police refused to tell relatives why the men had been arrested or where they were being held.

Finnish Americans began to whisper about towns-people who had turned in their friends, hoping to save their own skins. The immigrants, who had been so open and trusting with one another, suddenly started keeping to themselves. But no matter how many people were hauled to the Gray House, Father's answer remained the same: "Innocent people have nothing to fear."

Jake was looking forward to the opening of school as a distraction from the rumors. He was anxious to show Mrs. Sippola and his other teachers how much his Finnish had improved.

But in August, Maija came up with an idea that changed Jake's plans. "Father?" she said one evening. "I've been thinking."

"That's good to hear," he teased.

"Don't tease," Maija said. "I've decided that if I'm going to be a Soviet citizen, I should learn to speak Russian."

"That's a fine idea," Father said. "I've heard you practicing with your friends."

"I could learn even faster in the Russian school."

"You may have something there." Father paused and thought. "And it might be a great help to your brother, too."

"I can barely pronounce the name of our street," Jake said. "Besides, I'm just beginning to understand Finnish."

"The teachers may put you back a grade to start with, but you'd catch up easily enough," Father said.

Jake turned to Mother, hoping for support, but she said, "I'm sure your friend Aarne would help you."

"But I'd never see my other classmates," Jake said.

"If you want to advance in this society, you need to know Russian," Father said.

Jake was grateful when Peter took his side, saying, "Russian is difficult enough for someone who's interested in the subject, Father. It might be better if Jake stuck with Finnish."

"No. In the long run, Russian will serve him better."

"But —" Jake was frantic.

"That is the end of this discussion." Father cut him off.

"But you've always said discussions are good," Jake said.

"Jaakko!" Mother said.

"I've made my decision." Father remained calm. "You should thank your sister for her forward thinking."

Maija grinned.

■　■　■

When Jake saw Aarne the next day, he asked, "How would you like to give me Russian lessons?"

"Are you joking?"

"Father's sending me to the Russian school."

"It's too bad I won't be able to help you."

"What?"

"Not that I wouldn't if I could, but we're moving back to Suomussalmi."

Jake stared. Not only was he being transferred to a new school, but he was losing his best friend as well.

On the morning that Aarne was leaving for Finland, he stopped to say good-bye. Jake offered Aarne one of his most valuable baseball cards, a Lefty Grove. "A going-away present for you to remember me by," Jake said.

"That's real nice of you." Aarne turned the card over.

Jake laughed. "You'd rather have my Napoleon Lajoie, wouldn't you? Even though the Lefty Grove might be worth money someday."

"Napoleon's always been my favorite." Aarne grinned. "Besides, a lefty like yourself should keep his Lefty Grove."

On his first day of classes at the Russian school, Jake was so upset that his stomach hurt. The building was new brick with tall windows, yet it felt cold like a hospital.

When Maija smiled and said "Good morning" in Russian to the principal, Jake wanted to tell her to stop showing off.

Jake was so mad at his sister that when the principal greeted him, he could only stammer "*Nyet*." As a result, he was assigned to sixth grade, only a year ahead of Maija.

Jake's teacher, Miss Tatiyana Mityonov, could have been Victor Karlov's twin. She was a stout woman with a dark face and enormous hands and feet. She always had a pointer in her hand. Whenever Miss Mityonov clomped down the aisles of the classroom, the students pulled their feet under their desks for fear of having their toes crushed.

After attendance was taken on the first day, the students were called to the gymnasium. The principal gave a speech summarizing the school rules. Then she announced, "We will begin the year by honoring the beloved leader of the Soviet Socialist Republic, Joseph Stalin." She nodded to the music teacher, who directed the students in a patriotic hymn: "We give thee thanks for the sun thou has lit. . . ."

As Jake listened to the foreign words, he was angry. Hadn't his family come to Russia to learn about Finnish culture? How many times had Father complained that the Finns on the Mesabi Range were treated as second-class citizens? Had Father's dream of a new Finnish state been swallowed up by the grand giver of light, Stalin?

SHOTS IN THE DARK

Though Father remained confident about the Makis' future in Russia, Mother began to share Jake's uneasiness.

One Sunday evening when Jake returned from the baseball field, Mother and Father were arguing. Mother was so angry that she never heard him open the door.

"Don't start again," Father said.

"Edith says that loggers west of town have seen army trucks driving into the forest after midnight," Mother said.

"That's idle gossip."

"But the loggers have heard shots, too, Arvid. And they've found freshly disturbed ground in the forest."

"Innocent men are safe in this country."

"Then tell me what the soldiers could be burying at night in the middle of the woods."

Jake studied hard at Russian school, and with Peter's help he began to master the tongue-tangling language. Miss Mityonov, who'd seemed so mean at the start of the school year, turned out to be strict but fair. Though her history lessons were sermons that preached Lenin's Marxism, she was an inspirational literature teacher. When she saw how hard Jake was trying, she placed him with his own age group in math and science, saying, "Keep working, Jacob, and you will soon catch up in your Russian studies as well."

One afternoon, Jake got home from school to find Edith Kesänen sitting at the Makis' table, crying.

"What's wrong?" Jake asked.

"Edith's husband was arrested," Mother said. "He drove to Matrosa yesterday to pick up a load of wood. Soldiers came. He and nine others were taken."

"Were they all Finns?" Jake asked.

Mother nodded. Jake had decided the Soviet government was punishing the Finns for Gylling's pro-Finnish policies.

When Father got home, Edith begged him for help. He nodded and said, "I'll do what I can."

As soon as Edith left, Mother asked, "Should we start at the Gray House or the Ministry?" She stopped and looked at Father. "You don't plan on doing anything, do you?"

"We know the Kesänens, Father," Jake said. "Can't you see that something evil is happening?"

"Jaakko's right," Mother said. "This is all very strange."

"It is out of our hands," Father said.

"Now you're sounding like that cold fish, Karlov," Mother said. "How can they call this the People's Republic, when they are putting all the people in jail?"

"The Party is taking steps to purify itself." Father spoke calmly. "Times like these are meant to test our faith."

Nearly every day Jake heard of another man being taken by the NKVD. Four boys from his class at the Finnish school had lost their fathers. And after a week of inquiring at government offices, Edith Kesänen still had no news of her husband.

THE
RED BROOM

The NKVD continued to detain people, yet Father insisted his family was safe. Finally, two events shocked him into changing his mind.

One was the arrest of seventeen of his friends at the ski factory. On that morning, only three men showed up out of a crew of twenty. Several of the men worked in the same department as Father and had helped fit Jake's skis. "Do you really believe all those men committed crimes against the state?" Jake asked.

For the first time, Father said, "I don't know."

The second thing happened only three days later, when

Hanna Seppi's husband, Juho, was taken away by the NKVD. Hanna was so upset that she pressed William into Mother's arms. "Would you watch him, please?" she said. "I've got to find out what happened to Juho."

Mother begged Hanna not to go, but she walked straight to the Gray House. When Hanna didn't return that evening, Mother and the children took turns caring for little William.

A week passed and there was still no word of either Juho or Hanna. Jake and Maija quickly became attached to the baby.

Their other neighbor, Edith Kesänen, still had no news of her husband. Edith ate little, even when Mother brought her meals, and she became so nervous that every noise made her jump. One afternoon, Mother asked Edith, "Would it be too much to ask if you could help us look after the baby?"

"But we like William," Maija said.

"Maija," Mother said, "would you please help your brother fill the wood box?"

"But —" Maija began, but Jake said, "Listen to your mother." And when they got out in the hall, he whispered, "Can't you see that Mother is trying to help Mrs. Kesänen?"

"What do you mean?"

"Caring for the baby will help take her mind off her missing husband."

"Oh," Maija said.

When Edith stopped by to visit the next evening, Father bounced William on his knee. As the baby giggled, Father asked, "Who could be so cruel as to separate a child from his mother?"

Jake turned to Father. "The same men who've been arresting honest citizens for the last six months."

Father was about to answer, when Maija said, "Look how cute." The baby smiled at Father and held out his hands, saying, "Papa."

Things quieted during the week before the Revolution Day celebration. On parade day, along with the usual speeches and athletic contests, Peter was scheduled to play his first solo with the orchestra. Father got the family to the Philharmonic Hall a half hour early, just as he had on the night the Karelian recruiter had spoken in Finntown. Jake often thought back to that meeting. If only he'd convinced Father to stay home.

The concert, including Peter's brief but brilliant solo, brought enthusiastic applause. "Did you hear my son?"

Father asked Mr. Ranta as the family waited in the lobby for Peter. "He's played like that since he was in grade school."

"He must get his talent from his mother," Ranta teased.

"That's true enough." Father laughed. "I couldn't play a player piano myself."

"I wonder what's taking him so long," Mother asked.

"Let the young folks celebrate," Father said.

Just then, one of Peter's orchestra friends ran into the lobby. "He's gone," she said, stopping in front of Mother to catch her breath. "The NKVD took him away."

"What are you saying?" Mother said.

"Peter and five others." The girl was breathless. "They arrested them. It happened so fast. A truck pulled up, and before anyone could think to speak they were gone."

"Arvid!" Mother turned to Father.

"I'm sure this is all a mistake," Father said.

"I'm going to the Gray House." Mother headed out the door.

"We should wait until morning, Annikki," Father called.

But Mother marched outside, followed by Father and the children. The NKVD headquarters was dark and silent. Jake recalled the first time Aarne had shown him the cold facade.

"It's no use this late," Father said, but Mother pounded on the front door.

"Don't, Annikki," Father said.

She kept pounding. "What right do you have to take my son?" she shouted. "What right?" Then she began weeping.

As Father held Mother in his arms, Jake saw a light flicker in the basement window. But when he looked again it was gone.

Instead of going to work the next morning, Father went back to the Gray House with Mother. When Jake got home from school, Mother was more upset than ever. "Can you believe the gall of that man saying, 'There is no record of your son's arrest.' The whole orchestra saw his men take Peter away."

From then on, Mother walked to the Gray House each morning. The answer was always the same: "We have no record of an arrest."

When Mother wasn't questioning the authorities, she kept herself busy cleaning their tiny apartment.

One afternoon when Jake got home from school, he said, "You're doing it again, Mother."

"What's that?" Mother was intent on scouring the coffeepot. Her scrub bucket was also out.

"How many times have you washed the floor this week?"

Mother finally looked up.

"And Father doesn't even like it when you clean the inside of his coffeepot," Maija said.

Mother set down her rag and stared into the sudsy water. "But how can I sit and do nothing with Peter locked up in a prison or — or worse." Tears suddenly streamed down her cheeks.

Jake and Maija both hugged Mother, but it took her a long time to stop her crying.

After two weeks of inquiries, Mother managed to meet with a man in the Gray House who admitted that Peter had been charged, under Article N 58, with counter-revolutionary activities and sentenced to ten years in a prison camp.

But when she tried to confirm the story at the Military Tribunal in Lenin Square, an official told her Peter's sentence was fifteen years for charges "that had yet to be specified."

"They are lying," she told the family that evening. "Every single one of them is lying."

"It takes time to correct bureaucratic errors," Father said.

"How can you talk about bureaucrats when your son may be dead?"

Father's answer was to write letters to government offices in Petrozavodsk, Leningrad, and Moscow. He also asked his friend Oscar Corgan for help. "Oscar's been transferred to a publishing house in Uhtua," Father said, "but he still keeps in contact with people in the government. If we are patient, we will prevail."

"What does prevail mean, Father?" Maija asked.

"It means to win."

"But how can we win, when no one knows where Peter is?"

"We must —" Father stopped. Jake waited for him to say that we must trust the system. Instead, he said, "We can only do our best."

Jake had always wondered what his uncle meant when he'd warned Father about the Red broom on the night of their going-away party. Now he knew. The Red broom was the Communist Party sweeping away anyone who spoke against its awful might. They demanded blind obedience, and they would not be satisfied until everyone who had the courage to speak his mind was gone.

TROIKAS

Jake heard boots marching on cobblestones. He reached for the watch that lay on the table beside his cot. In the moonlight, he could see that it was a quarter past two. Jake had slept fitfully since the night that Peter was arrested. Today they had received more bad news. Oscar Corgan's wife, Katri, had written to Father and reported that her husband, too, had been taken into custody.

Since the NKVD night squads traveled in groups of three, people called them *troikas*, the Russian word for threesomes. The *troikas* followed the same route each time they passed Jake's home. Though the exact day could never be predicted, the sound of their boots, marching in the deepest quiet of the night, was always the same.

Despite the muffling cold outside tonight, the boots were louder than usual. At suppertime, the temperature had dropped to twenty below zero. By dawn it would be forty below or colder.

As Jake listened to the stones ringing under the marchers' heels, the scent of wood smoke and stale cabbage drifted in from the hallway. Jake knew the pattern all too well. The pounding would get louder and louder until it sounded like the boots were coming through the wall. Only then would it begin to fade.

Directly across from Jake, Father breathed deeply. Jake wondered how he could rest knowing that no one was safe. Carpenters and accountants, teachers and journalists, had all been arrested. Most of the men had been Finns, but lately they were picking up other nationalities. Even women were no longer safe. The other evening they'd arrested a Finnish-American opera singer down the street. Refusing to go quietly, she woke the entire block by singing the Soviet national anthem as they led her away: "Boundless is my motherland beloved. Thousands are the rivers, lakes and woods . . ." her voice echoed in the darkness. "Here you breathe as freely as you should!"

144

Suddenly Jake realized that the marching had stopped. In the brief pause that followed, a voice barked a command. The boots turned toward the barracks. Jake held his breath.

When the door creaked below, Jake whispered, "Father! Mother!"

"What is it?" Father rolled over. "Why aren't you —" Then he heard the men on the stairway and sat up. By now the whole building was shaking. Mother clutched Father's arm. Maija leaned forward in her bunk and stared at the door.

The boots passed by the first apartment. If they only kept going, Jake prayed. If —

All at once the marchers halted. A fist hammered on the door. "Open in the name of the People's Republic," a hoarse voice commanded.

"Just a moment," Father said. He pulled on his pants and lit the kerosene lamp on the table. Summoning all his dignity, he walked to the door and opened it. "May I help you?"

A short man wearing a sable cap stepped inside. For a moment he was taken aback by Father's politeness. Then he wiped the frost from his mustache and sneered, "Is there an author in the house?"

Jake was unnerved by how kindly the man looked. His

face was thin and ruddy-cheeked, and his brown beard neatly trimmed. His eyes were calm and gray. *If he were wearing a robe,* Jake thought, *he could pass for a youthful priest.*

"You must be mistaken," Father said. "There is no author that I know of in these barracks."

"I see." The man turned as if he were about to leave. Instead, the man at his side handed him a packet of papers.

"Did you not write these?" He held out a pile of Father's letters. Jake could see the Lönnrot logging camp address on one.

"Yes, of course. But —"

"You are under arrest." His voice cracked like a whiplash.

"There must be a misunderstanding," Father insisted.

"Is your name Arvid Maki?"

"Yes, but —"

"And are you an employee of the ski factory?"

"I tell you this is a mistake," Father said. "I have been a loyal member of —"

"We do not make mistakes," the man interrupted. "Get dressed." Then he motioned for his partners to search the apartment.

Jake watched in disbelief as the men went through their family papers, taking birth certificates, passports, letters from America, photo albums, Mother's Hudson's Bay blanket, and even Jake's baseball cards and the .22 rifle that he'd won.

"Why are you doing this?" Mother's voice trembled as she pulled her robe tightly around her shoulders. "We have a right to know."

Instead of answering her question, the man turned toward Jake. "And how old might this young capitalist be? I didn't see his name on my list, but if he proves himself to be an enemy of the people, I'm certain we will find him out."

"How dare you threaten —" Mother began.

"Yes," Maija shouted, "you leave my brother —"

"Annikki! Maija!" Father quieted them. "I am certain that this matter will be resolved shortly."

"But, Arvid —"

"Please," Father said, stepping toward the dresser.

Mother was shaking so badly that she had to sit down on the bed. Jake reached down to give her a hug, but she buried her face in her hands to stifle her sobs. Maija stood stiffly, crying to herself.

While Father buttoned his shirt, the men stuffed the things that they had gathered into two pillowcases.

Father picked up his gold pocket watch, but the man said, "It would be best to take something less valuable."

He pointed toward Jake's stainless steel watch. "Perhaps that one."

"But why —" Mother started again.

"Everything will be fine, Annikki." Father unhooked his chain and handed the gold watch to Jake. Then he picked up Jake's watch. "You don't mind if we trade, do you?" he said, running the worn leather strap through his belt loop. "Just temporarily, of course."

Not trusting himself to speak, Jake nodded.

Father whispered, "*Sisu,* my dear," to Mother as he stepped forward and clapped Jake on the shoulder. "You look after the ladies until I get back," he said, "and make sure you don't wind that watch too tight."

Then he was gone.

Mother sat back down on the edge of the bed. Rocking slowly, she stared at the yellow lamp flame. Mother squeezed Maija's hand and tried to blink back her tears.

Jake stood at the door and listened to the sound of the boots receding. He reached into his pocket and touched the case of the gold watch. It was still warm from Father's hand. Jake hung on to the echo of the marching as long as he could, hoping against hope that the sound would turn and build again.

FRIENDS IN THE NORTH

The day after Father's arrest, two letters arrived from Jake's friend Joe. It had been a year since Jake had heard from Minnesota, but he was in no mood for news about baseball.

Jake stared at Joe's address, growing more angry by the second. No doubt the government had intentionally released these letters today to show how much they controlled his life.

"Aren't you going to read them?" Maija asked.

"Two can play at this game," Jake said, leaving the unopened letters on the table.

Following Father's arrest, Jake expected Mother to visit

the Gray House or to go on a cleaning spree. Instead, she only sat in her chair. "I knew it was a mistake to come here," she said, staring at the one small window in the room.

"There was no stopping Father," Jake said.

"I should have spoken up. It felt so wrong. Fortune delivered a pearl into my hands that gave me a good life in a new land. But I might as well have cast that gem back into the lake and never left Finland." Then she was crying. "Forgive me for such talk, Jaakko. That would mean —"

"I know what you meant, Mother," Jake said.

Mother was so distracted that she didn't even play with little William when Edith came to visit. And no matter how hard Jake and Maija tried to cheer her up, they had no luck. One afternoon, Jake sang a folk song in his tuneless voice, hoping Mother would join in, but she didn't even smile.

Mother's sadness forced Jake and Maija to be strong. He and his sister prepared the meals and picked up the house. When Mother did ask, "How was school today?" or "Is it cold outside?" she really didn't listen to their answers. Even when Mother picked up her knitting, the needles that normally clicked so brightly lay silent in her lap.

As much as Jake missed Father, he was even more

lonesome for Peter. Peter had always been the calm, steady one. Whenever Jake got impatient or upset, Peter would chuckle and say, "Take a breath, Hub. There's always tomorrow."

But as the arrests continued, tomorrow was the very thing that Jake most feared. Though a few of Jake's neighbors were lucky enough to be warned before the NKVD came, most people still hung packs behind their doors and were ready to leave at a moment's notice. One family hid in the frozen woods each night for a week, waiting until the *troikas* had come and gone.

For some reason, if the NKVD found your house empty, they rarely returned. A bachelor from the ski factory slept under an overturned boat by the lakeshore all of October rather than risk going home. Another family returned from vacation to find their house boarded up, but when they moved back in, no one bothered them.

For those who weren't forewarned, arrests could happen anywhere and anytime. The immigrant houses known as the *Välibarracks* were the most frequent targets, but no quarter of the city was safe. Twenty men could be taken one night and none the next. To Jake, it seemed like the moment a person got too confident, the NKVD would arrive on their doorstep. People younger than eighteen were rarely taken, but it happened often enough to keep them in fear, too.

Now that Jake was sixteen, he knew the odds were increasing that his turn would come. If only there was some way to predict when and where it would happen. The NKVD might never stop at their apartment again, or they might keep coming back until they had arrested every single person in the building.

Living with the fear and doubt, Jake could almost understand why some men chose suicide rather than facing up to the terror of the *troikas*. Since Jake didn't know where to turn next, he visited Mr. Ranta one day.

"How nice of you to stop by, Jaakko," Ranta said. "I'm so sorry to hear about your father."

"That's why I've come," Jake said. "I've heard there are ways people can help relatives who've been arrested."

"This is true," Ranta said, lowering his voice. "Can I trust you to keep a confidence?"

Later that week, Mr. Ranta called on Mother. "Thank you for receiving me," he said, taking off his hat.

"Please have a seat." Mother smoothed back her uncombed hair. "Would you like some coffee?"

"No, thank you."

"Jaakko told me that you had important information to share," Mother said. "Have you heard anything of Arvid or Peter?"

"I am sorry to say that I have not, Mrs. Maki."

"I was hoping —" Mother hung her head.

"Of course you were." Ranta nodded. "But I do have other news which may be of interest. As you know, things are becoming more dangerous for foreigners every day."

"This isn't news, Mr. Ranta."

"That is why I have come. There is a way you could take Jaakko and your daughter to safety."

"What are you saying?"

"I have friends in the north who have been helping people find their way across the border to Finland."

Mother stared at Mr. Ranta. "Are you suggesting we escape?"

"The choice is yours. But there is a grave risk in staying."

"And what if Arvid returns?" Mother asked.

"In the event that your husband or son shows up, we would get word to you."

"We can't go away and leave Father!" Maija cried.

"Hush, Maija," Mother said, her eyes coming to life for the first time since Father had been taken away.

"Feel free to take some time to think about our

conversation," Mr. Ranta said. "In the meantime, please keep this between us. Trust is a rare commodity these days." He pushed back his chair and took his hat in his hands. "I should warn you that there is no telling how much longer we can keep our little underground railroad open. The dangers are great for those who are involved."

"Why would you do this for us?"

"I was an immigrant like you. In 1931, I came from Fort Frances, Canada, with big dreams and a bad case of 'Karelian Fever.'" He smiled sadly. "Besides, Arvid was a good friend. He knew it was dangerous to question the authorities, yet he wasn't afraid to speak freely. I don't have Arvid's courage, but I made a solemn promise to help you if something ever happened to him."

PART III
THE DARKEST
EVENING OF
THE YEAR

DECEMBER 1937
THE NORTH

NIGHT TRAIN

I'm not going!" Maija said.

"You can't do this," Jake said, "not after all our planning." Now that they were finally ready to leave, Jake was afraid that Maija might convince Mother to change her mind.

"Father said innocent men have nothing to fear," Maija said. "He'll come back soon. I know he will."

"How can you believe that nonsense?"

"Not so loud, Jaakko. Please," Mother said.

"It isn't nonsense!" Maija shouted. There were tears in her eyes. "Father did nothing wrong. The men in the government will find their mistake." Maija threw herself down on the bed and sobbed. "We can't go away and leave him all alone."

Jake grabbed Maija by both wrists. "Father is not coming home." Maija turned her head away and kept crying. "Do you hear me?" Jake shook his sister. "Stop sniffling and look at me. He's not coming home. Not now. Not ever."

Maija stared at Jake as if he had slapped her.

"I'm sorry, but we need to hurry or we'll miss the train."

Maija refused to speak the whole time Mother and Jake finished packing. The last thing Jake did was pull out the last two letters that he'd received from Joe, and he placed them on the center of the table, still unopened.

"Why are you leaving those?" Mother asked.

"I want to show the NKVD that I know what they're up to," Jake said.

Mother frowned. "Is it wise to antagonize them?"

"What more can they do to us?" Jake said.

After they boarded the train to Kem, Maija turned toward the frosty window and sat in silence.

Mother took Maija's hand and said, "Your fingers are cold." But Maija refused to speak. That suited Jake just fine. As long as she was quiet, they had a chance of succeeding. He and Mother had been getting supplies together for the last month, and Mother had sewn coveralls from the white sheets she'd saved the whole time they'd lived in Karelia. The hardest thing was saying good-bye to Hanna Seppi's baby, William. Edith Kesänen had been helping Mother care for him, and she agreed to take over full time. Edith admitted that the baby was the only thing keeping her sane since her husband had disappeared.

Mr. Ranta had contacted a friend in the north and sent three pairs of skis and poles ahead. Ranta said that skiing across the border was the safest way. Soldiers watched the roads leading into Finland, but they couldn't patrol the vast wilderness that stretched all the way to the arctic. Jake's family would not know the identity of their contact until they met him at the Kem station. "How will we know who it is?" Jake asked.

"They will know you," Ranta said. "But if by some chance the time is not right, you must return to Petrozavodsk."

The last time Ranta stopped by their house, he'd warned Jake that speed was the key. "Your government travel permits allow you to be gone three days," he said. "You'll lose one day traveling to Kem. That gives you two days' head start on the NKVD." Jake wanted to ask Ranta what would happen if they were caught, but he knew. After the interrogation, they would be beaten, and prison camp or worse would follow. "Luckily, you are a fast skier."

As the train rattled north toward Kem, Maija fell asleep. But Jake's mind wouldn't rest. He kept thinking through their plan, hoping that they hadn't overlooked anything. He couldn't help recalling the recruiter back in Finntown who'd promised them an education free to all. Though a Russian education might not cost anything in dollars, it was by no means free. For there could be no freedom in schools that taught every subject through Lenin's twisted vision of Marxism.

The morning was still and dark when the train pulled into Kem. Jake had forgotten how short the winter days were up north. Jake helped Mother step onto the station platform, but Maija snatched her hand back angrily.

Jake searched the crowd of fur caps and frosted mustaches for a likely face. But no one looked in their direction.

While they waited, a man in a ragged coat stopped next to Maija and lit a cigarette rolled out of newspaper. Could their contact be disguised as a vagrant so he wouldn't draw attention to himself? Jake recalled the day in Leningrad when he'd first caught the stench of newsprint and cheap tobacco. In his mind, the smell had come to stand for that hopelessness known as *nichevo*.

When the smoke drifted into Maija's face, she coughed and said, "Yuck."

The man was ready to say something, until Mother scolded Maija. "Treat others as you wish to be treated."

"I'd never burn garbage in someone's fa —"

"That's enough," Mother silenced her.

Jake worried that Maija was drawing too much attention to them. One by one the passengers picked up their bags and climbed into old cars and horse-drawn sleighs. Had their contact decided to cancel?

Suddenly a policeman in a greasy fur hat appeared. "Are you waiting for someone?" he asked, speaking the Karelian dialect of Finnish they'd used in Lönnrot.

"Yes," Jake said, and without thinking he added, "We are visiting a friend for Christmas."

"Christmas?" The officer scowled.

"And Father Frost's Day," Jake added, knowing it had been a mistake to mention the forbidden Christian holiday.

"These look like fine packs." The policeman tapped the leather strap of Jake's pack with his wooden stick.

"It's called a Duluth No. 2," Jake said. "They're specially designed for canoe trips." What if the man asked to see inside? One look at the white suits, and their plan would be undone.

"Very heavy canvas," the policeman said, bending to touch the outer flap. "And fine stitching. I enjoy camping myself."

The policeman was hinting he would leave them alone if they gave him one of their packs as a bribe. Otherwise, they would be taken to the station for questioning. The train depot was now empty. Jake's hunting knife was tucked in the outside pocket of his pack. Could he bring himself to reach for it?

Just then, a man stepped onto the far end of the platform and waved. "Look." Jake pointed. "Our ride is here."

When the man came closer, Jake's hopes fell. It was Victor Karlov! Karlov's dark eyes narrowed as he approached them. He was probably working with the police.

"Hello, my dear," Karlov said in an extra-loud voice, walking up and embracing Mother. "So sorry I'm late." Then Karlov shook Jake's hand. Still speaking loudly, he said, "Welcome to Kem, my boy." Then he turned to the officer. "If you'll excuse us?" He touched his cap. "The car is this way."

Karlov picked up Mother's pack for her, and Jake grabbed his and Maija's. As they walked down the street, Karlov whispered, "Don't look back. These petty fools won't ask questions if you show confidence." Then raising his voice, he said, "So tell me, how was your train ride?"

Karlov didn't speak again until he had driven clear of the city. "My farm is near Paanajärvi on the Kemi River."

"But why would you ever —" Jake stopped.

"Why would I help you?" Karlov smiled.

Jake nodded.

"If I seemed distant at Lönnrot, I was only looking out for myself. In this society, you never know who you can trust. I've seen children turn in their own parents to the police. When you first meet people, you have to follow the Party line. One wrong word can put you in the gulags."

"So you're not a communist?" Mother asked.

"Certainly not," Karlov said. "I've been a farmer my whole life. When the government started to collectivize the farms, they claimed people donated their land. The truth was, if you didn't give up your farm, it was seized. You were declared a greedy kulak and forced to leave your home."

"Father said that the kulaks were rich," Jake said.

"I'm peasant stock," Karlov said. "To prevent the

government from taking my farm, I joined the rural development committee. My assignment to Lönnrot was as close as I could get to my home and my wife."

"Your wife?" Mother said. "Then you were separated from her the whole time?"

"I managed to sneak home a few times each year. But we didn't have it as bad as some. I know couples who were assigned to jobs a thousand miles from each other. The Party does not believe in family. They say that personal attachments weaken your devotion to the socialist cause."

"How cruel," Mother said.

"Cruel and stupid," Karlov said. "When the purges began, I tried to help as many people as I could."

"We are grateful," Jake said.

"It takes careful planning, but things look good for you. The full moon should offer perfect skiing conditions."

"You mean we're skiing into the woods at night?" Maija spoke for the first time.

Karlov glanced back at Maija with a worried look.

"We're going to follow Mr. Karlov's advice," Mother said, patting Maija's arm.

"Do we have a long drive?" Jake asked.

"I would recommend getting some sleep," Karlov said.

Karlov's old Ford was in worse shape than the car the

Makis sold before they left Minnesota, but every mile they drove was a mile they wouldn't have to ski.

Jake tried to rest, but his mind was still reeling from their close call at the train station. Mother was wide awake, too, but Maija had fallen fast asleep.

Just as Jake finally dozed off, Karlov tapped his arm. "If you would please duck your heads." Karlov stared straight ahead. "It's probably only a logging truck, but we can't be too careful."

Jake heard an engine winding. Karlov reached down and pushed a blanket toward him. "You'd best cover up," he said. Jake pulled the blanket over his head. The truck sounded like it was driving right at them.

Karlov suddenly swerved toward the ditch. "Fools," he muttered as he wrenched the wheel back to the left.

"What's wrong?" Maija cried, waking out of a sound sleep.

Karlov coasted to a stop so he could gather himself. "That was close," he said. His engine idled roughly. "It was a military truck. They nearly ran us off the road."

"A truck with soldiers?" Mother had sat up.

Karlov nodded. "They're probably hauling political prisoners to Kem. From Kem, they ship them to camps in the north and east. They even hold some people on islands."

Jake thought of his father. Perhaps he'd been lucky enough to end up in a prison camp.

They met a farm truck a few miles later, and from then on it was an empty road, bordered by snowbanks and dark stands of tall pine. When they drove through a small village called Kepa, Karlov swore under his breath. Jake wanted to ask if it was the police, but he kept his head down. A moment later Karlov explained, "It was my nosy cousin Svetlana. She waved for me to stop, but I pretended not to see her."

On the outskirts of Paanajärvi, Karlov pulled over. "I want to show you what's become of Salo's equipment." A sign in the headlights read SALO-MAKI SAWMILL. Beyond it Jake saw piles of stacked lumber in the moonlight.

"You've named the sawmill after them?" Mother asked.

"It's only fair since Arvid and Ed did all the work," Karlov said. "Besides, it makes for a good joke when new customers come in and ask, 'Are you Salo or Maki?'"

Just a few miles farther on, Karlov pulled into the driveway of his farm. He shut off his engine and looked back down the road. Then, still checking over his shoulder, he said, "This way." He ushered them into the barn and lit a lantern. "The farm was started by my grandfather in 1852."

Karlov's home was a three-section log building

consisting of a house, hay barn, and cow barn, all joined together. Jake saw Maija wrinkle up her nose at the manure smell, and he was afraid she was going to say something. "Whose idea was it to connect the buildings?" Jake asked. "I've only seen one other house barn like this at the Seitiniemi farm in Wasa Township."

"My father came up with the plan. But before we go inside, let me show you something." He walked to the far corner and held out his lantern. Maija jumped when a mouse darted past her toes and dove under a mound of hay. Leaning against the wall were three pairs of skis. "The Gylling factory's finest," he said. "And they're waxed with your father's special mixture."

When Karlov opened the door, he was greeted by his wife, who looked accusingly at him, as if to say, How dare you risk our lives for these strangers?

Before Karlov could introduce his guests, a dark-furred animal jumped up from beside the woodstove and dashed at them.

Maija dropped to her knees.

"Be careful!" Karlov said. "She snaps at —" He stopped.

"Medved," Maija squealed.

"I forgot how much she likes you." Karlov smiled. "She won't tolerate anyone going near her or her pups."

"Pups?" Maija looked up as she ruffled Medved's ears.

Just then, three little puppies got up from a blanket in the corner and waddled over to Maija.

As Maija petted the puppies, Medved whined softly. "Are you teaching your babies to be bear hunters?" Maija looked into Medved's eyes, and the dog barked.

Karlov chuckled, then he turned to his wife. "May I introduce my wife, Irina?" The kerchiefed lady nodded stiffly, but she didn't speak. "This is Mrs. Maki, Jake, and Maija."

While Maija played with the puppies, Karlov helped Jake and Mother set their packs down on the worn plank floor. Then he walked to a drawer and pulled out a folded piece of paper. "I've mapped your route." He flattened the paper on the kitchen table. "To start, you'll follow the Kemi River. Then you'll head north, keeping clear of the *Liikasenvaara* border road." He traced a line with his finger. "Once you cross this logging road, a westerly heading will take you past Haikola. It's only a dozen houses, but you can't risk being seen. Who knows if a trapper or a lumberjack might be tempted by the NKVD bribes for turning in escapees?"

"How much money do people get?" Jake asked.

"The official bounty is fifty rubles, but the usual payment is one sack of flour."

"They trade a life for a sack of flour?" Mother asked.

"Times are tough. From here" — Karlov placed his finger on the map — "the border will be less than one hundred miles away. The last village to avoid is Pistojärvi. The Finnish Frontier Guard has been arresting suspected Russian agents at the border, but you will hardly look like spies."

Jake studied the last line Karlov had drawn. A hundred miles would be a two-day trip if he was traveling alone. He'd often skied twenty-five miles in an afternoon with Aarne. But Jake was worried about Mother and Maija. Mother might have *sisu*, but she was not an experienced skier. And Maija was so moody.

"If you ski hard tonight, you'll get clear of the logging road I mentioned. From then on, it should be safe to travel during the day, though we get precious little light this time of year. Fires, of course, can only be lit at night."

"Of course," Jake said.

"But what if we get cold?" Maija asked.

"You must be strong," Karlov said.

Maija made a sour face, but she didn't say anything more.

Mrs. Karlov served boiled cabbage and potatoes. Though Jake had trouble spooning down the watery soup, he knew this would be his last home-cooked meal for a week. He vowed that once they made it to Finland, he'd put his cabbage-eating days behind him.

After supper, he and Mother opened their packs and checked through the items one last time: six loaves of bread, a sack of oatmeal, some tea, three tin cups, one small cooking pot, a metal canteen, six wool blankets, a canvas tarp, ski wax, a hatchet, a compass, a hunting knife, two lengths of rope, and three boxes of waterproofed matches.

Mother picked up the package of tea and smiled sadly. "Your Father preferred coffee on his camping trips, you know."

"He always made us lug that big copper pot," Jake said.

"I like coffee better, too," Maija said.

Jake portioned out the supplies so most of the heavy things were in his pack. Mother and Maija would carry two blankets each, along with matches and a loaf of bread in case one of the other packs got wet.

"I can carry more than this," Mother said.

Jake shook his head. "I've skied the most."

Just then, Mrs. Karlov surprised Jake by holding out a small cloth sack and a jar of jam to Mother.

"Irina would like to offer you some dried lingonberries and jam for your trip," Karlov translated.

"*Spasibo.*" Jake spoke for Mother, using the Russian for thank you.

"Before you go," Karlov said, "let me show you something." He opened the bedroom door, and there stood the Makis' bed. "When I didn't hear from you, I brought it here for safekeeping."

"Our plans for a larger home fell through," Mother said. "I hope you can make good use of it."

"Folks still call it the American bed," Karlov said.

Blinking back her tears, Mother said, "I suppose we should get started."

"That would be wise," Karlov said.

They put on their coats, and Mother pulled out the white suits that she'd sewn. "My sheets have finally come in handy."

"You've planned well." Karlov touched the drawstring that Mother had attached to Jake's hood. "You'll be hidden as well as rabbits against the snowdrifts."

Lifting a pack in each hand, Jake stepped into the blue Karelian night. He shivered as the cold crept down his neck. Steeply angled moonlight washed the snowy field and the birches in silvery white. A tall spruce beyond the barn cast toothed shadows over their faces and arms.

"We'd be in trouble without the moon," Jake said.

Karlov nodded. "During the darkest evenings of the year, we have to plan our travels around the phases of the moon."

Jake thought of Frost's "Stopping by Woods . . ." If only they had a horse and sleigh like the man in the poem to carry them to the border.

As they buckled on their skis, a howl followed by a series of sharp yelps echoed from the hills beyond the house. Medved barked once and peered toward the woods.

"Was that a wolf?" Maija asked. Her eyes were so wide that they reflected little bits of starlight.

"They're miles away," Karlov said.

Jake helped Maija and Mother adjust their packs. Then he shouldered his own. He was surprised to see Karlov putting on skis. "I'll take you upriver to the point you turn north," he said. "From there you'll have to break your own trail."

"At least the weather's not too cold," Jake said.

"Perfect for skiing," Karlov agreed. "Ten degrees or so."

"It feels freezing to me." Maija huddled down.

"It could be fifty below this time of year, especially with the full moon," Karlov said. "Follow me." He planted his poles and kicked forward on his skis. Medved trotted beside him.

A gentle downhill grade led across a glistening field toward the Kemi River. When they reached the bank, Jake was amazed to see a packed ski trail. "My neighbors and I keep this open during the winter," Karlov said. "It makes for quick travel between our farms."

The moon was a near-perfect globe above the jagged pines as they skied up the frozen river. The night was so clear that Jake could see Karlov's breath rise over his tall fur cap and settle in a fine, white frost on his shoulders. The longer Jake was outside, the more his eyes adjusted to the darkness. Soon the landscape seemed as bright as a cloudy afternoon.

Jake was glad to see that Mother and Maija kept pace, staying only a stride or two behind.

At a curve in the trail, Karlov turned and watched. "I knew Jake was a fine skier, Mrs. Maki, but you do well yourself."

"My grandfather spent his life skiing after his reindeer herds. I must have winter traveling in my blood."

"And she's got *sisu*." Jake smiled.

"Of course," Karlov said. "I'd forgotten that you're a Kuusamo girl. This trip will be a homecoming for you."

Mother nodded. "If only —"

"If only it were a happier time, I know." Karlov paused. "Unfortunately, we must part here."

"We're as ready as we'll ever be." Jake pulled out Father's watch and checked the time. It was midnight. He snapped the watchcase shut. The gold cover was warm from his pocket. He thought back to the boots of the *troika* and the night that Father had handed him the watch.

"From now on, it'll be bushwhacking for you," Karlov said, leading the way up the bank. Jake smiled. Bushwhacking was the term skiers used when they broke their own trails. During his last winter in Minnesota, Jake and his friends had bushwhacked a trail all the way from Finntown to Lookout Mountain.

When they reached the north side of the river, Karlov stepped out of his skis and snapped off a pine branch. "Stay clear of the roads," Karlov said. "I'll cover your tracks back to the river. After one snow, there'll be no trace." Jake caught the sharp scent of fresh pine sap. "When you cross that logging road, I'd suggest you brush over your tracks."

"I don't know how we can thank you enough," Jake said, slipping off his mitten and shaking Karlov's hand.

"Arvid was —" Karlov said. "I mean, Arvid is a good man. It's the least I can do for him."

"You've risked so much," Mother said, extending her hand. "It was brave of you to help."

"I wouldn't call it something so grand," Karlov said. "Any man with a conscience would do the same."

"Thanks again," Jake said, turning toward the woods as Medved barked a last good-bye to Maija.

BUSHWHACKING

With his first few strides, Jake could tell that the going would be much harder in the woods. Luckily, the snow had crusted over during a recent thaw, leaving only six or eight inches of fresh powder to plow through.

Marking his course by the North Star, Jake skirted the deep shadows of the pine stands. The stars were paler than Jake was used to, and the familiar constellations of Orion and Taurus were so close to the horizon that they were hard to identify.

Jake stopped often to check his compass bearings. Every time he paused, Maija said, "I'm thirsty."

"We should save our water, dear," Mother said. "We

won't have any more until we can start a fire and melt some snow."

"I'll eat snow then." Maija scooped a handful of powder into her mouth and let it melt.

"Don't chill yourself," Jake warned.

"I'm steaming hot." Maija loosened her scarf.

Jake wove through the brushy forest of birch and pine. As the moon swung higher, the white land brightened. When he paused on a hillside, Mother said, "I've never seen shadows so clear."

"Can I have a drink now?" Maija sighed.

"Once our canteen is empty we won't be able to fill it for a long time," Jake said.

"Why didn't we stay in Petrozavodsk?" Maija threw her hood back. "We could get all the water we wanted there."

Mother pulled the canteen out of Jake's pack. "Just a sip," she said, but Maija took a big drink.

The water cheered up Maija, and she was soon going so fast that her ski tips were riding over the backs of Jake's skis.

"Can't you go any faster?" Maija asked.

"It's a long way to Finland," Jake said.

"I thought you were a ski racer," Maija said.

When Jake started down a low hill, he warned Maija to

slow down, but she toppled into the snow, giggling. Jake pulled her up quickly and brushed her off.

"Why are you so worried about a little snow?" Maija said.

"It's important you don't get wet," Mother said.

"But the snow feels good," Maija said, touching her cheek.

Jake shook Maija's mittens off. "Would you listen to your mother for once?" he said.

Tears suddenly ran down Maija's face. "I didn't want to go on this trip anyway."

"Don't cry." Mother patted Maija's eyes with her hanky.

"Why couldn't we wait for Father?" Maija kept crying. "How will he feel when he comes home to an empty house?"

Jake looked back toward the Kemi and shook his head.

After Maija settled down, Jake led the way through an open field flooded with moonlight. "It looks like it's all sprinkled with jewels," Maija said.

When they got to the far side, Mother said, "Let's have a slice of bread for a snack."

Following their rest, Maija said, "I'll race you." She sprinted ahead of Jake, calling, "Slowpoke," over her shoulder.

"I told you to pace yourself," Jake scolded her.

"You're just mad you couldn't catch me." She pulled off her cap, and steam rose from her head.

"Your brother is worried that if you get too warm, you'll become chilled later," Mother said.

In order to reach the next ridge, they had to cut through a swamp that was crisscrossed with fallen trees. The shadows made it hard for Jake to see, and the snow was so soft that he sank halfway to his knees with every stride.

As Jake cleared the way for Mother and Maija, pine branches caught on his pants and ski poles.

In the middle of the swamp, Jake found his path blocked by fallen trees. "We can backtrack," Jake said, "or we can take off our skis and climb over them."

Mother said, "There's no guarantee we'll find a better route." The wolves howled again in the distance.

Jake unbuckled his bindings and helped Mother and Maija with theirs. In the deep snow, it was hard for Jake to keep his balance with his skis and poles slung over his shoulder. As he climbed over the first tree trunk, his ski tip hooked on a branch and he fell sideways into the snow.

"Make sure you don't get all wet," Maija teased.

As angry as Jake felt, he didn't say a word.

When they finally got through the swamp, everyone was panting. Jake pulled out his watch to check the time. "It's already a quarter to five," he said. "If we don't reach that logging road soon, we'll have to find a place to camp."

A clearing lay ahead. On the far side stood a spruce grove. Jake worried that he'd veered off course in the night.

"I'm tired," Maija said, looking out from under the white hood that she had pulled down to her eyebrows. "And I'm cold." She'd buttoned up her coat, but she couldn't stop shivering.

"We told you it was dangerous to get too hot," Jake said.

"Why?" Maija asked. "Will the wolves find us?"

"I just meant we need to be careful," Jake said. "It's not as if we can step inside and warm up by the woodstove."

Mother slipped off Maija's mittens. "Your hands are like pieces of ice."

"They feel like needles are poking me," Maija said.

Jake said, "I'll ski ahead and check out that grove. You follow along when I wave."

"Be careful," Mother said.

Jake pushed ahead, glad to be on firmer snow again. When he reached the dense spruce thicket, he decided it would be a perfect camping place. He waved a ski pole to signal Mother.

While he waited for Maija and Mother, Jake took off his skis and packed the snow at the base of a big spruce. Then he broke off smaller branches and made a bed. Before they went to sleep, he would lay the horse blanket over the boughs, and they would cover themselves with their other blankets. He wished the NKVD hadn't taken Mother's Hudson's Bay blanket.

When Mother and Maija arrived, his sister was still shaking. If skiing across the clearing hadn't warmed her, Jake knew she must be very cold. "I'll build you a fire," he said.

"That would be nice." Maija's voice quivered.

"Though we can't risk anyone seeing the smoke after dawn," Jake said, "we should have plenty of time to warm ourselves and melt some water for tea."

Jake gathered birch bark and dry branches. By the time he got back, Mother had scraped away the snow with one of her skis. A single match started the pile crackling. Soon a bright blaze was steaming their coveralls and mittens dry. "We're going to smell like a smoke sauna," Mother said as Maija huddled down beside the flames. Jake piled more boughs beside the fire to make a seat, and he helped Maija slip off her boots. Her socks were wet and cold. Though Jake was wearing Peter's waterproof leather boots, Maija's *huopikkaat*, or one-piece felt boots, got wet easily. "Hold your feet by the fire," Jake said, rubbing her toes to start the circulation.

"They feel all tingly," Maija said.

"Don't get too close to the flames," Mother said.

After Maija's socks were dry, Jake got out the cooking pot to melt snow. "I'll fill our canteen first," he said. "Then we can boil some oatmeal for —" Jake stopped. "What was that?"

"I didn't hear anything," Mother said.

Jake stepped away from the fire and listened. There it was again. A far-off scraping.

Jake ran back to the fire. He grabbed the nearest ski and raked snow over the fire. Then he stomped out the hissing embers with his boots. Mother and Maija looked confused.

"Are you crazy?" Maija moaned.

"Hush up," Jake said. The scraping was coming closer. And it was accompanied by a jangling sound.

"Who cares if I talk way out —"

"Shut your mouth," Jake hissed.

When Maija quieted, Mother whispered, "Sleigh bells?"

Jake nodded. Along with the bells was the scraping of the iron runners of a logging sled.

For a moment, it sounded like the horses were going to walk right into their camp. The animals were so close that he could hear the clomp of their shoes and smell their sweat.

When the sound finally began to fade, Jake said, "That must have been the water wagon."

"What do they water?" Maija asked.

"They pull a big wooden water tank to ice the ruts so the horses can pull the logging sleds more easily."

"My feet are still cold," she said.

"We've got to get your boots back on," Jake said. "It's too risky to stay this close to the road."

"You said we could eat," Maija said.

"Later," Jake said. He knelt to fill the canteen from the cooking pot. Then he rubbed the sides of the blackened pot with snow to clean it and stowed it in his pack. "We should all take a drink," Jake said, offering the canteen to Mother first.

When it was Maija's turn, she made a face. "Yuck. This tastes like ashes."

"That will give you extra energy," Mother said.

"I'll bet those loggers would let us warm up in their bunkhouse," Maija said.

"Right before they turned us in to the NKVD," Jake said.

The road was less than a hundred feet from their camp. "I should have scouted ahead," Jake said. "They would have seen us as soon as daylight came."

Mother nodded. "It was pure luck that the smoke from our fire was drifting the other way."

Rather than risk crossing in an open place, Jake found a spot where they had to push through some underbrush. Before he stepped onto the ice road, he peered in both directions. Then he waved Mother and Maija across, and walked backward after them, sweeping a branch from side to side.

Jake knelt to help Maija buckle her straps. "We'll start another fire and eat breakfast just as soon as we put some distance between us and that road."

For once, Maija was too tired to complain.

MILES TO GO BEFORE WE SLEEP

Jake took his bearings and headed north. Now that he'd found the logging road, he was more confident of his directions. Jake pushed hard, pausing only long enough to read his compass and to check on Mother and Maija. Though Mother was keeping up, Maija was moving more slowly all the time.

When Jake stopped at the top of a low hill, Maija said, "Can we rest now?"

"This might be a good time to have a slice of bread." Jake slipped off his pack and took his hunting knife from his belt.

"Can we try Mrs. Karlov's jam?" Maija asked.

"Let's save the jam until we can toast our bread for dinner," Mother said. "That will give us a treat to look forward to."

Maija didn't reply.

The moon finally set at eleven in the morning. "Isn't the light strange?" Jake asked, peering into the milky gray haze.

"It's like an out-of-focus picture," Mother said.

"The sun will be up any minute," Jake said, astonished at how different this frozen gray world was compared to the midnight sun that had greeted the Makis on their first evening at Lönnrot.

"Let's eat," Maija said.

Jake sawed off a piece of bread and handed it to Maija.

"Aren't we going to toast it?" she asked.

"We can't risk a fire until after dark," Mother said. "Drink some water. That will help wash it down."

By the time they'd finished their lunch, the first hint of dawn streaked the eastern sky.

"Time to get trekking," Jake said.

"My legs are sore," Maija complained.

"So are mine, little sister," Jake said. "Ski racing is nothing compared to breaking trail in this brush. But we'd better take advantage of the sun."

"What sun?" Maija said. "There's nothing but grayness."

Though the sun barely rose above the horizon, the sky gradually brightened to a snow-sparkling blue. At sunset, Jake stopped on the side of a ridge and watched the thin red clouds in the distance. Maija said, "It's like smoke and flames all mixed together."

Jake pulled out his watch. "Only two-thirty, but it will be dark very soon."

Mother turned to Maija. "You know what that means?"

"The wolves are coming?"

"Don't be silly. Once it's dark, we can build a fire."

"And then we can have hot bread and jam," Maija said.

"That's right."

By the time Jake chose a sheltered area to camp, a cloud bank was moving in from the west and gradually blocking out the moon and the stars.

"Snow could be heading our way," Mother said.

"That will be perfect for covering up our tracks." What Jake didn't say was that a snowstorm could also slow them down. They had only a week's supply of food. If the

NKVD hadn't taken his rifle, he could have shot rabbits and squirrels.

Jake turned to Maija. "Ready for your toast and jam?"

"I'm too tired to eat," she said.

"Let's get those skis off," Jake said.

"We'll boil a nice pot of tea," Mother said. "That will make you feel better."

Maija looked ready to cry. Mother loosened Maija's right ski binding while Jake undid the left.

Once Jake started a fire, Maija's mood improved enough for her to enjoy a cup of tea and some toasted bread with jam.

Mother's eyes got misty when she tasted the tart lingonberry jam. "Arvid loved winter camping," she said. "If only he and Peter could be here with us."

Jake nodded. "Father always joked that he wanted to go back to your old village and visit the land of the short people."

"There are a few tall ones that would have surprised him."

"You mean that WILL surprise him," Jake said. "Once we get across the border, we'll write so many letters to those politicians in Petrozavodsk and Moscow that they'll deliver Father in person."

NIGHT-BLIND

Jake woke to a black sky and the smell of cold ashes. There was no North Star. No Big Dipper. It was totally silent. He blinked and saw nothing but gray. Snowflakes tickled his forehead. After sleeping in the same clothes that he'd skied in, Jake felt cold and clammy. His hands were sticky with dried sweat and dirt, and his woolen underwear itched. Trying not to disturb Maija and Mother, Jake tilted his watch and squinted at the numerals. Maija, her head tucked far under the blankets, snored beside him.

"What time is it, Jaakko?" Mother whispered.

"Four o'clock. We may as well let her sleep."

The branches crunched under Mother's hips as she turned over.

When Jake checked his watch again, it was five-thirty. Maija never stirred until Jake had melted a pot of snow. She peeked out from under the snow-covered tarp and rubbed her eyes. "I was hoping this was all a dream."

"Come and sample my famous snow porridge," Jake said.

After breakfast, Jake checked his compass. It was snowing so hard that he had to brush the snowflakes off to read the dial. "That's west." He pointed into the dim, moonlit haze.

"Where's the sun?" Maija asked.

"It won't be up until just before lunch," Jake said.

Jake and Mother shook the snow off the blankets and rolled them up. Then they strapped on their skis and started out.

Jake's skis were hushed. The fresh snow, which had sparkled under last night's moon, was a dull gray. Jake paused beside a birch.

Mother blinked and stared. "The trees look like they're draped in a black veil."

"My shoulder hurts," Maija said.

"Where?" Mother said.

Maija pointed under her right pack strap.

"Let's have a look," Mother said, helping Maija slip off her pack. She unbuttoned Maija's coat and pulled down the neck of her sweater. "There's a sore spot on your collarbone."

"Am I bleeding?" Maija asked.

"It's just irritated."

"I'll get some padding," Jake said, taking off his pack and pulling out a red handkerchief, which Mother folded over the sore.

Jake helped Maija lift her pack back in place.

"Does that feel better?" Mother asked.

"A little," Maija said.

They started off again. The snow was still falling. Jake's legs ached from the day before. Though he was in good shape, the weight of his pack and the effort of plowing through deep snow had worn him out. He skied forward, squinting in the dim light. Gray trees blended into gray sky and gray snow. Jake planted his pole, and a birch branch poked him in the face. He jerked back.

"Are you all right?" Mother asked.

"I'm fine," Jake said, pressing his cold mitten into his

eye, "but we have to find more open country. There's supposed to be a river south of here." He pulled out his map, and Mother lit a match while he looked. As the sulfur smell of the match drifted up, a wolf called from the ridge behind them.

"They sound close," Maija said.

"They're more scared of us than we are of them," Jake said. "The light should be better on the river, and we wouldn't have to worry about getting lost."

"Do you think it would be safe?" Mother asked.

"If we stay in this brush, we could ski right off a cliff."

Jake led the way from one open patch to the next. Once a rabbit darted past Maija, and she squealed. When Jake got to the river, he checked his watch. "The sun should be up in an hour, but I don't see a hint of light."

"It must be the clouds," Mother said.

"My shoulder hurts," Maija said. When Mother looked at the sore spot again, she found that Maija's skin was bleeding.

"I'll carry your pack for a while," Jake said, strapping hers on top of his own. Jake was glad to see that the river followed the northwest course that Karlov had plotted on his map. Even a small error in direction could send them north toward the arctic barrens or south to the NKVD.

The snow continued. When they stopped for a mid-morning snack, Maija asked, "When is the sun coming up?"

Jake opened his watch. "It already rose. But the clouds are blocking most of the light."

The farther upriver they went, the more rugged the country became. As the dim shape of rocky cliffs came into view, Jake was glad they had taken the river route. Skiing those slopes would have been impossible in the poor light.

At a sharp turn in the river, Jake stopped and listened. At first he thought he heard a machine, but as the snowflakes ticked against his hood, he said, "It sounds like a rapids."

Mother looked worried. "There'll be thin ice then."

Knowing Mother's fear of bad ice, Jake said, "We'll hike around it. The south shore looks like the easier climb."

They took off their skis and clambered up the boulder-strewn hill beside the rapids. Jake stopped at the highest point and looked down on the rushing river. Steam plumes rose from the channel, and the black rocks were bearded with glistening ice.

"It's beautiful," Maija said, the roar of the rapids turning her voice to a whisper.

"And terrible," Mother said, leaning backward.

In the middle of the afternoon, the snow began to taper off, and the sky turned a soft pink.

"Why don't we stop for a snack?" Jake said, brushing the snow off a fallen log beside the river. He made a seat from pine boughs while Mother got out the rye bread and canteen.

By the time they'd finished eating, the snow on the river was glimmering with starlight, and the moon had risen above the trees. "At least we won't have to worry about getting lost between now and bedtime," Jake said.

"Don't say bedtime," Maija said. "It makes me sleepy."

The next morning, Jake woke up shivering. A cold front had blown in during the night. The black, skeleton branches of the birch trees rattled above his head. And their white coveralls, which Jake had hung across a pine branch to dry after supper, whipped in the moon shadows like the loose-clad arms of a scarecrow.

Jake squinted at his watch. It was only three A.M. He huddled under the blankets, but he couldn't stop shaking.

An hour later, Jake gave up trying to sleep. His boots were so stiff that he had to stomp down hard before he could wriggle his feet in. Shaking from the cold, Jake knelt to light some birch bark. The wind blew down his neck and made him shiver even worse. His first match broke in half, and the second one slipped out of his fingers and fell into the snow.

Jake cupped his hands and blew on his fingers before he tried again. A blaze was soon crackling. The cold stung his hands every time he took off his mittens to add snow to the cooking pot. Despite the noise and the smoke, Maija and Mother didn't stir until Jake had filled the canteen and made the tea.

By the time they finished breakfast, the wind was even stronger. Jake headed upriver, fighting gusts that hit him square in the chest and stopped his skis in midglide. He felt like a boxer pummeled by a constant rain of blows, fighting to keep his balance. To make conditions worse, loose snow blew across the river ice and pelted his face.

"Stay close behind me," Jake yelled to Mother and Maija, trying to shelter them from the worst of the wind.

"I'm cold," Maija whined. But it did little good when Mother stopped and doubled her scarf across her face.

The wind finally began to ease when it was time to make camp for the night. "Will it be calm like this tomorrow?" Maija asked, touching her windburned cheeks.

"I'm afraid so," Jake said, checking his map and finding that they'd only gone half as far as the day before.

"What's there to be afraid of?"

"Your brother means that if it stays clear tonight it is going to get very cold," Mother said.

"Colder than today?"

Not wanting to frighten Maija, Jake said, "There's always a chance that clouds might move in, and it won't get too bad."

THE BIG CHILL

The next morning, a sharp chill prickled Jake's face. It was perfectly still. Moonlight washed over the forest, leaving the shadows of birch and pine etched on the snow. Jake sat up. A dull throbbing pounded in his head. Before he could reach for his boots, Mother startled him.

"It's too bad we don't have a mirror," she said, peering over her blanket.

"Why?" Jake's voice was hoarse.

"Your eyebrows are covered with frost."

Jake brushed his finger across his brow, and flecks of frost fell into his lap. Jake picked up his boots. "They feel like wood." He tried to put on his right boot, but even

197

when he stood up, he couldn't jam in his foot. He grabbed a stick of wood. Sitting down on the blanket, Jake whacked the sole of his boot hard, driving it onto his foot.

"What's that?" Maija shouted, sitting up.

"It's only Jaakko, dear," Mother said.

Maija frowned at Jake. "Why is he hitting his foot?"

After Jake pounded on both his boots, he lit a fire and jogged in place until his feet warmed. Then he heated Maija's and Mother's boots beside the fire.

When Maija stood up, she scurried to the fire. "How cold do you think it is?" she asked.

"Thirty or forty below."

After breakfast, everyone helped break camp. Mother cleaned the oatmeal pot and cups with snow, Maija rolled up the blankets, and Jake waxed the skis.

Jake led the way upstream. The air was so dry and cold that his skis squeaked just like they had in Lönnrot on cold mornings. Even with his scarf pulled across his face, the cold burned Jake's skin. And his fingers ached inside his mittens.

As the hills got steeper, their detours around rapids became more difficult. Jake dreaded taking off his mittens to reach into his pocket, but he had to check the map. According to Karlov's route, their course should take them across a small lake and past the headwaters of two rivers near Pistojärvi. If Jake didn't find the lake soon, he would have to risk a cross-country heading.

Maija's feet were so cold that they had to stop and build a fire. "The smoke will show for a long way," Jake said, "so you'll have to warm up quickly." He brushed the snow off a rock for a seat, and he built a fire, using the driest wood he could find. Jake's hands were numb by the time he'd slipped off Maija's boots and propped her feet on a small log in front of the fire.

Jake walked down the bank to get more wood, when Maija yelled, "Help!"

Jake ran back. Maija had dropped her sock into the fire. Jake flicked the burning sock into the snow, but the toe was already burned off.

"If I'd only brought some yarn for darning," Mother said.

Maija was crying now. "I'm sorry, Mother."

"That's all right, dear." She kneeled to comfort her.

Jake didn't say anything, but he was worried. Now Maija would need a fire every few miles. Why hadn't they thought to bring more spare clothing?

When they started again, Jake's compass showed the river was veering north. By midafternoon, Jake was ready to bushwhack a path to the west, when he heard the sound of running water. Around the next bend was a rapids and just above it, the lake.

"Finally," Jake said.

"It's lucky we were patient," Mother replied.

Jake nodded. Though finding the lake proved that they were on the correct route, it also meant that they were less than halfway to the border. With more rough country ahead, they were down to two loaves of bread and one cup of oatmeal. Another problem Jake had to face was the waning moon. Less light meant less travel time. And the more slowly they traveled, the faster their food would run out.

RUDOLPH'S ROAD

When they struck inland from the lake the next morning, the temperature began to rise. Jake hoped to make up for the time they'd lost during the cold spell, but the hills beyond the river were so steep and rugged that they spent more time climbing over rocks than skiing. And despite the warmer weather, the hole in Maija's sock made her foot so cold that they had to stop twice to build a fire.

At the edge of a tangled swamp, Jake knelt beside an animal trail. "These tracks are too big for deer."

"See those clumps of moss?" Mother pointed to a pawed-up patch of ground under the pines.

"Deer don't eat moss."

"No, they don't." Mother smiled. "But reindeer do. And it looks like they've packed a trail for us."

"Maybe they're Finnish reindeer going home," Maija said.

"Let's hope so," Jake said.

Thanks to the reindeer trail, they crossed the headwaters of the second river on the following afternoon. When they stopped to build a fire, Jake pulled out his map. "According to this," Jake said, "we still have a long trek to the border."

As Jake set up camp that evening, Mother took him aside. "Do you realize that we're nearly out of bread?"

"I know." He nodded.

"Is there some way you can snare a rabbit?"

"If only I'd thought to bring some wire or fish line."

"Why aren't you starting a fire?" Maija called. "I'm cold."

Just after sunrise on the following morning, Jake was trying to decide if the tracks of the reindeer herd had turned too far north, when he saw a flash of brown. He crouched and peered through the brush. "What is it?" Maija asked.

Jake waved his hand to quiet her. "Something's feeding on a carcass," he whispered. When the animal lifted its small rounded head, Jake was glad to see that it wasn't a wolf. "It must be a fox cleaning up a reindeer kill."

"Can we save the reindeer?" Maija asked.

"If we can scare that critter off, we're going to eat it."

"Not a reindeer!" Maija said.

"Yell and wave your hands," Jake said, skiing forward. As he got closer, he saw a bushy brown tail, but the animal kept its head down. Jake wondered why a fox would be so bold. When he was close enough to see the freshly killed reindeer yearling, Jake lifted his ski pole and shouted even louder.

The animal whirled. It wasn't a fox or a wolf but a snarling wolverine. Jake had heard stories of these creatures called *carcajou,* or woods devils, but he'd never seen one. With a fierce growl, the wolverine charged. Its fangs were bared, and the fur on its back and tail stood straight up. Jake expected the animal to bluff an attack and stop. Instead, it leaped straight for Jake's throat. The last thing Jake saw before the wolverine hit him full in the chest was a streak of silver between its black weasel eyes.

As Jake fell backward, he swatted the wolverine in the shoulder with his ski pole. The animal somersaulted into the snow. Jake heard Mother and Maija screaming. Their voices sounded far off, but by the time Jake had scrambled to his feet, Mother was standing beside him and waving her ski pole at the wolverine. "Get away!" she shouted. "Get!"

Still snarling, the wolverine looked ready to attack again, but Mother threw her ski pole and hit it in the nose. Only then did it bound away through the deep snow, stopping to stare one last time at the creatures who'd robbed it of its meal.

"Good throw," Jake said.

"What was that?" Maija said.

"A wolverine," Jake said. "I've heard they're mean enough to chase wolves off a kill."

When Jake got out his knife, Maija said, "You're not going to cut up that poor reindeer?"

"This meat is fresher than anything you could buy in a butcher shop," Jake said.

Maija wrinkled up her mouth.

While Jake skinned the hindquarters, Mother built a fire. Then he cut some of the meat into thin slices and hung them over a pole, suspended above the fire by two forked sticks. "We'll smoke these nice and slow," Jake said.

"The jerky should last the rest of our trip," Mother said.

"But for now we'll try a nice, thick steak." Jake sawed off a slab of meat and pierced it with another forked stick that he held close to the flames. The roast meat smelled delicious, but Maija refused to take even one bite. Instead, she nibbled on the last piece of bread and sipped a cup of tea.

When it was time to stop for the evening, Maija looked pale. The rough country and the cold were wearing her down.

Jake was looking for a campsite when he spotted what looked like a house. He signaled for Maija and Mother to stay back. But after peering around the trunk of a shaggy spruce, Jake saw a log platform, built about ten feet in the air and covered with a birch-bark roof.

"It looks like an old hunting stand," Mother said.

"At least we've found ourselves a shelter," Jake said.

"We're not climbing up there!" Maija said.

"No." Jake smiled, looking at the cracked log ladder. "We'll just lay our beds underneath it."

Though Maija limped on her sore foot, she did her best to help collect firewood and make a pine-bough bed. When Jake roasted more meat for supper, Mother handed a small piece to Maija. "Try a little, dear, please. You need to keep up your strength." Jake feared if his sister didn't eat, she would become too weak to ski. Luckily, she took a small piece along with her tea, and her color soon looked better than it had for two days.

ENEMIES OF THE STATE

Sometime during the night, Jake woke to a sudden flash of light and a grinding sound. Fighting the urge to jump up, he lay still and listened. The clutch of an old truck made a clanking sound as the driver downshifted to climb a hill. The engine clattered loudly as the truck accelerated.

Jake remembered the fire. He turned over. The flames had fallen to embers. If he threw on snow, there would be a rush of steam and smoke. He decided it was safest to lie still. Brakes screeched, and the engine stopped. Could it be soldiers on night patrol? Should he risk waking Mother and Maija so they could sneak deeper into the woods and hide?

When the truck doors opened and slammed shut, Maija rolled over with a start, but Jake clamped his hand across her mouth. "Quiet," he whispered.

Suddenly a chorus of voices rose in the darkness. "Where have you taken us?" asked an angry Finnish man.

A Russian shouted, "Enemies of the people have no rights." Jake saw that Mother had awakened. He motioned for her to lie still.

"Get out!" another Russian commanded.

Jake heard scuffling followed by a moment of silence. Then a voice said, "Kneel, border hoppers."

"You have no right to —" The words were stopped by a pistol shot. Maija jerked in her blankets and let out a cry that Jake muffled with his hand. The shot was so loud that the muzzle must have been pointed straight toward them. Before the echo of the first blast had faded, a second shot was fired.

Jake and Mother hugged Maija tightly, but they couldn't still her trembling. A last Finnish voice shouted, "Lenin is a harlot's son and a dog!"

"Capitalist!" was the one-word reply.

After the final shot, the woods were silent except for the crunching of boots on snow. Then low voices mumbled something in Russian. The only words Jake heard for sure were "fools" and "dreamers." The truck doors creaked open and slammed shut. Only after the truck drove off did Jake finally breathe again.

"Who were those men?" Maija's voice shook.

"Soldiers or NKVD," Jake said.

"Like the *troikas*?"

Jake nodded.

After they lay quietly for a few more minutes, Mother whispered, "What should we do?"

Jake looked up at the half-moon. "It's bright enough for us to move on," Jake said.

But before Mother could reply, Maija started snoring. "There's our answer," Mother said. "She needs to rest."

Jake checked his watch at five A.M. Moonlight sparkled on the open patches in the trees. Mother and Maija were still asleep. Before he lit the breakfast fire, Jake resolved to do a thing that he dreaded.

Less than a hundred yards away lay a frozen creek bed. The only signs of last night's murders were the bodies and a single set of tire tracks that stopped on the far side of the creek. Three men lay on top of the snow. Each had his hands tied behind his back. By the marks in the snow, Jake could tell that they had been forced to kneel before they were shot through the temple. The boot prints showed that one man had jumped up and run a few paces before he was gunned down.

Jake dreaded going closer, but he knew how desperate Maija was for a pair of socks. He walked up to the body that lay apart from the rest. Avoiding the man's face, Jake untied the frozen boot laces and tugged off the man's boots. As he reached for a sock he saw that a piece of paper had fallen onto the snow. Jake uncrumpled the hastily scrawled note.

To: Kari Sarinen
Aurora, Minnesota

Dearest Sister,
There is not much time. We were nearly to the border when the soldiers caught us. I don't know where they are taking us, but I fear the worst. No matter what happens, I can't say I wasn't warned. Tell Mother the mistake is all my own.

Eero

P.S. The others with me are Makela from Iron River and Koski from Negaun —

The last word was cut off. Jake wondered what sort of a man Eero Sarinen had been. Aurora was a small Iron Range town. The dead man's eyes looked up through frost-covered lashes, and his half-parted lips were frozen in a final condemnation of Stalin.

Jake was wondering if his father had had a chance to write a note, when Mother called, "No, Maija. Don't."

Jake turned. His sister had run down the creek bank. "Don't look," Jake said. But Maija's eyes were locked on the corpse. Jake stepped forward to shield her. Her face was as white as the dead man's. "Let's go back to the camp," he said.

"Why would anyone do this?" Tears streamed down her cheeks.

Jake wasn't sure what to say. "At times men are ordered to do hateful things," he said, "and they are too weak to say no."

"Your brother is right," Mother said. "We mustn't let evil poison our hearts."

Maija pushed them both away. She looked at the bodies and then at Jake. "They did this to Father, didn't they?"

"No —" Jake stopped. "There's no telling for sure. They may have taken him to a prison."

Maija shook her head.

"People can live for years and years in prison," Jake said.

"You're just saying that."

Jake took her by the shoulders. "We must never give up. Do you hear me?" Maija fought back her tears. "The only way we can ever find out what happened to Father and Peter is by getting to Finland. From a free state, we can pressure the Russian government for information. It's our only hope."

Maija suddenly calmed. "So we owe it to Father and Peter to make it across the border?"

"That's right." Jake nodded.

Maija turned toward Mother. "We'd better have breakfast, then, so we can get started."

Jake was impressed by the intensity in Maija's eyes. For the first time since they'd left Karlov's farm, she looked anxious to begin the day's trek.

THE RUT RACE

Do you think it was wrong to borrow that man's socks?" Maija asked.

They'd been skiing all day, but this was the first time Maija had mentioned the dead man's socks. "I'm sure he'd be proud to help you," Mother said.

Jake stopped suddenly.

"What's wrong?" Mother said.

Jake motioned for Maija and Mother to crouch down. Then he slipped off his skis and crept forward. Only a few yards ahead was a cutting, bordered by an ice road.

Jake walked back.

"What is it?" Mother asked.

"A logging road and a clearing," Jake said.

"That means there must be a logging camp nearby," Mother said. "Can we risk crossing the road?"

Jake turned to Maija. "How are your legs holding up?"

"I'm tired."

"I think it's time we tried a little quicker style of traveling," Jake said.

"Surely not the road?" Mother asked.

"We've got to move faster," Jake said. "Once we lose the moonlight, we'll only be able to travel at midday. And our jerky won't last forever."

Before Mother could say anything more, Jake pulled out his watch. "In an hour, the loggers should be heading in for dinner. That ice road heads straight west. If we ski down —"

"But what about the water wagon?" Maija asked. "Like we saw before?"

"They never start icing until after supper. Let's wait a minute and see."

A short while later, Jake heard the scrape of sled runners and sleigh bells as a team pulled a load of logs past. Jake said, "I'll bet that's their last run of the day."

"What if you're wrong?" Mother looked worried.

"If we hear another sled, we'll ditch into the woods."

"But —"

"We'll travel ten times as fast as in the woods." Jake turned to Maija. "Are you ready for a downhill run?"

"You mean we could just coast?"

"That's right," Jake said. He placed his right ski in the ice rut. "I'll show you the way." Jake angled his left ski in the middle of the road to act as a brake. "If you're going too fast, tip your left ski out like this to slow you down."

Maija smiled. "It will be nice to not have to pole."

"But you have to promise to be quiet. Okay?"

"Okay, Jake."

Jake looked over his shoulder to make sure the road was clear. "See you at the bottom," he said. One push sent him flying down the hill. His right ski hissed in the ice rut and his left ski threw up a tiny plume of snow. Compared to plodding through the woods, Jake felt like he was going a hundred miles an hour.

When Jake got to the bottom, he waved for Maija.

Maija was soon racing so fast that her hood blew back and her blond hair whipped out from under her cap. Her open mouth told Jake that she wanted to squeal, but the only sound Jake heard was the whizzing of her skis.

When Maija hit the flat at the bottom of the hill, she almost tipped backward, but she kept her balance and coasted all the way to the base of the gentle rise where Jake stood.

"Wheeew!" Maija gasped.

"Was it fun?"

She nodded.

"Look. Here comes Mother."

The fresh tracks helped Mother ski even faster. Wide-eyed, she shot across the flat and coasted right past Jake and Maija, who tried hard not to laugh out loud.

By following the logging road over a half dozen hills, they covered more ground in two hours than they had all day. Once they got to the end of the road, Jake made sure that they brushed over their tracks and skied clear of the logging area before they made camp. By then it was so dark that Jake had to rely on starlight to find an open area to lay out their bedrolls.

THE CROSSING

The next morning, Jake woke to a perfect silence. The hazy arc of a crescent moon hung low over the trees, and the air was still. When Jake sat up, fresh snow fell from his blanket. The sky was so dark that he couldn't see the face of his watch until he lit a match. It was six-thirty, the latest he'd slept during their entire trip.

A gentle snowfall continued as they prepared breakfast and all through the morning. The closer they skied to the border, the more often Jake stopped to check his compass bearings.

"Can't we go faster?" Maija urged.

"We've got to be careful, as gray as it is. We don't want to make a wrong turn now that we've come this far," Jake said.

Jake was sure they must be near the Finnish border. Today would be ideal for a crossing. Though the snow made it difficult to plot their course, it would make it equally hard for the Russian border guards to see them.

The sun finally rose at eleven, just as the pale, waning moon was setting. Despite the steady snow, the sun lightened the sky enough for Jake to see a series of pine-topped ridges in the west.

When they stopped for lunch, Jake said, "We must be close, but if we can't find the border soon, we'll have to make camp."

"Wouldn't that be dangerous?" Mother asked.

"We should be safe if we don't build a fire."

"No fire all night?" Maija looked ready to cry.

"I'd like to keep going," Jake said, "but the moon won't be up until after midnight, and we can't risk traveling blind."

Jake was about to give up hope, when he saw an opening in the trees. "This could be it," he whispered to Maija and Mother.

They skied to the edge of the woods and stopped. A road lay directly ahead. Jake checked his compass and smiled. "It runs north-south, just as I'd hoped."

"So Finland's right over there?" Maija pointed her ski pole.

"It's only a long fly ball away." Jake smiled. He peered up and down the hill through the gently falling snow. The road was empty. "No sense wasting time." Jake unbuckled his skis and broke off a pine branch to cover their trail. "Are you ready to give it a try?"

Mother and Maija nodded.

"You start, and I'll follow right behind." Holding his skis and poles under one arm, Jake walked backward, brushing over their ski tracks as quickly as he could.

When they reached the road, Jake was glad to see fresh snow in the ruts. That meant no traffic had passed this way for a long time. Mother stopped and stared to the west. "I can't believe we've made it." Her voice trembled.

Jake glanced up at the lifting clouds. Now that the snow had stopped falling, the brightening sky made him nervous. He knew they wouldn't be safe until they reached the cover of the forest again. "Let's keep moving," Jake said. "I'll cover up the rest of our tra —"

Just then, Jake heard a truck downshifting to climb a hill.

"What's that?" Maija looked frightened.

Jake's mind raced. "We'll make better time if I break the trail," he said, bending quickly to buckle on his skis. "Let's kick hard."

Jake skied as fast as he could, checking over his shoulder every few strides to make sure that Mother and Maija were keeping up. As they neared the woods, he heard a truck door open behind them. Jake looked back. Two soldiers jumped out with rifles.

Maija turned, too.

"No!" Jake shouted, but it was too late. Maija's ski tips crossed, and she tumbled into the snow.

One of the soldiers raised his rifle and aimed toward them. Jake was kneeling to take off his skis and help Maija, but she scrambled to her feet on her own.

"No!" Jake yelled again. But Maija threw back her hood and pulled off her cap. Her blond hair spilled down.

"Stay low!" Jake yelled.

"We've got to keep going." Maija gripped her ski poles tightly and stood tall. "They'd never shoot a little girl."

Jake's mind whirled. Should they take cover behind a snowbank or continue sprinting for the woods? "Keep going, Mother," Jake said.

"But —" Mother began.

"Ski!" Jake shouted, waving her forward.

As Mother kicked past him, he spoke to Maija. "Stay as close behind me as you can," he said.

Jake turned. The trees were less than twenty strides away.

"*Ostanovites*," a Russian voice called. Jake knew that meant "halt." Then a harsher voice added, "Halt, or we will shoot."

Jake heard the metallic snap of a bolt-action closing.

"Hurry," Jake called to Maija. "Hurry."

The first, softer voice spoke again, saying, "*Ona tol'ko devochka*. She's only a girl."

"Halt," the harsh voice commanded. "Halt, I say!"

Mother had reached the edge of the forest by the time the first shot was fired. She stopped to look back, but Jake yelled, "Keep going!"

When a second blast echoed down the ridge, Jake glanced back, afraid he would see Maija bleeding in the snow. But her hair was flying off her shoulders, and she was still skiing hard. Jake wondered how the soldiers could miss from such close range.

As Jake turned toward the woods, a third bullet whined over his head. When he saw a tiny puff of snow high in the crown of a pine tree, he knew the soldiers were trying to scare them by shooting over their heads.

"Keep skiing," Jake called.

The closer Jake got to the woods, the lower the soldiers fired. By the time Jake reached the first spruce tree, a bullet ripped into the black bark only a foot above his cap.

"Head for that thicket," Jake called to Mother.

In a few more yards, they would be screened by the brush. Jake turned. One of the soldiers had walked partway down the hill and leveled his rifle again. By the flash of sun off the scope it looked like the muzzle was aimed directly at them. Jake dodged behind the tree and reached for Maija's coat sleeve. Just as he pulled her toward him, a bullet smacked into the opposite side of the tree. That shot had been meant to kill.

"Jaakko!" Mother shouted.

"Don't stop now!" Jake yelled.

Maija was flushed and panting. "Keep going," Jake said. "Straight for those trees."

"Be careful, Jake," Maija said.

"I'll be right behind you. If he aims this way again, I'll yell for you to duck. Go now." Jake pushed her up the trail.

As Maija started out, Jake felt for the knife on his belt.

He knew he would have little chance if the man came after him, but he wasn't giving up without a fight. Jake peeked around the spruce. When he saw that the soldier hadn't moved, he followed Maija, glancing over his shoulder to make sure that the tree stayed between him and the soldier.

Finally, the other soldier shouted from the top of the hill. "We must not trespass on Finnish soil," he called. "Come back immediately."

Jake breathed deeply for the first time since he'd heard the truck. He'd never heard anything sweeter than those two simple words: Finnish soil.

"Jaakko," Mother called from a thicket. "Are you all right?"

"I'm on my way."

When he caught up with Mother and Maija, they were hiding behind a big pine. Mother reached out and squeezed him tight. "Thank goodness you're safe."

"We've got Maija to thank for that." Jake turned to his sister.

"She was a very brave girl," Mother said.

But Maija suddenly started crying.

"What's wrong?" Jake asked.

"I might have looked brave when those soldiers were shooting at us," Maija said, "but I was shaking inside."

"We all were," Mother said.

"Really?" Maija asked.

"Really." Jake grinned.

Jake looked up the hillside. He didn't need his compass to know that he was facing due west. At that moment, Jake felt a surge of hope.

"How does it feel to be home?" Jake turned to Mother.

"Home?" Mother looked confused for a moment. Then she smiled. "Yes, I suppose I am home. If only Arvid and Peter were with us." Her eyes teared up again.

Jake looked back toward the border one last time. "Now that we're finally here, we can begin our most important journey."

"Another trip?" Maija looked ready to cry again. "Haven't we gone far enough?"

"I don't mean a journey on skis," Jake said. "I mean the journey that will lead us to the truth of what happened to Father and Peter."

"Father would like that," Maija said.

"And so would Peter," Mother said.

Jake nodded. "And we won't rest until we get the

answer." After a moment of silence, Jake said, "We'd better keep trekking."

"It would be nice to find a town before dark," Mother said.

Jake pointed up the hill. "Let's see what's over that ridge."

By late afternoon another cloud bank had moved in, and it was getting difficult to see. When they paused for a drink, Jake studied the sky. "We'll have to make camp if we don't come across a road or a village soon," Jake said.

"Look," Maija called. Jake skied to her side. A small clearing lay just ahead. In the middle of the opening was a road and a pile of logs. Fresh tire tracks showed that a truck had recently passed by. "If we shout, there might be loggers close enough to hear us," Maija said.

"Just wait," Jake said, taking out his compass. "I want to make sure we haven't wandered off course with all these clou —"

Just then, a sharp bark pierced the twilight. Jake looked up and saw a dark shape bounding toward them. Though the animal sounded like a dog, it was large and black and had the pointed ears of a wolf.

"Watch out, Maija!" Mother shouted from behind.

Jake kicked off his skis and stepped in front of his sister.

"Don't, Jake!" Maija yelled.

"Stay back," Jake said, planting his boots in the snow and pointing his ski pole forward. As Jake braced himself, he could see that the charging animal wasn't a wolf but a huge German shepherd with its fangs bared.

When Jake heard a man shout from beyond the log pile, he feared the worst. The Russian border patrol must have returned with a guard dog to hunt them down! Jake readied his sharp-tipped pole. As fast as the animal was charging, he would have only one chance to spear it.

"Don't hurt him, Jake." Maija pushed past her brother. "He's only a dog."

"No, Maija!" Jake grabbed at her sleeve, but it was too late. She stepped between him and the dog.

"Hey, boy," Maija called, holding out her hands. Jake barely had time to turn his ski pole aside, before the dog hit Maija and knocked her backward into his legs. As Jake and Maija toppled over, Mother let out a scream. Jake grabbed for his knife handle, but by the time he'd pulled the blade from its sheath, the dog was diving for Maija's throat. One snap of those jaws, and it would be over. Jake was just about to plunge his knife into the shoulder of the dog, when he stopped. To his amazement the giant creature was only whining softly and licking Maija's face.

"Stop that." She giggled, pushing the dog away. "You're heavy."

Now Jake heard another man shout. This time the words sounded Finnish. A tall man skied up with a rifle slung over his shoulder. He stopped and stared down at Jake and Maija. "Can you believe it?" he asked.

A shorter, darker man who'd just caught up to his partner shook his head and said, "That dog usually makes meat out of anyone he gets ahold of."

"You're not Russians?" Mother had reached Jake's side now.

"Of course not. We're Finnish Frontier Guard. And I take it that you're not spies?"

"Spies?"

"Our main job is to keep Russian infiltrators from sneaking across the border, and Surmaaja" — he pointed at the dog — "is our helper."

The second man was still staring at Maija. "Your little girl has made quite an impression on Surmaaja. He never takes to strangers that way."

The tall guard nodded. "Last week, he tore up a big

Russian fellow so bad that we had to carry him out on a stretcher."

"My daughter has a special touch with dogs," Mother said, helping Maija and Jake to their feet and brushing the snow from their clothes.

"I can see that," the second guard said.

The tall guard turned to Jake and asked, "So how far have you folks come?"

"We —" Jake paused. "We started in Minnesota."

"You've had yourselves quite a hike then." He smiled and extended his hand. "Welcome to Finland."

HISTORICAL NOTE

The man behind the "Karelian Fever" exodus was Edvard Gylling, an expatriate who fled Finland after the Finnish Civil War of 1918 and settled in Russia. An active member of the Communist Party, Gylling soon won Lenin's confidence and was placed in charge of Karelian recruitment. Gylling's grand vision to build an independent Finnish republic in Karelia was an irresistible temptation to many idealistic and adventuresome Finnish Americans who were living in the midst of the Great Depression and were confronted daily with massive unemployment, poverty, and a general sense that capitalism had failed.

At first, things went well for the new arrivals. A spirit of optimism and cooperation prevailed. The Finns applied their skills and enthusiasm to construction projects, logging operations, commercial fishing, and factory work. The results were immediate and impressive.

However, by the mid-1930s Joseph Stalin had seized control of the Soviet Union, and he soon decided that the democratic-minded Americans and Canadians represented a challenge to his dictatorial authority. Stalin ordered a series of purges to "purify" the Communist Party. These so-called purges ultimately rewarded the well-intentioned immigrants with illegal arrests, torture, imprisonment, and execution. Thus began a dark time that has since become known simply as the Terror.

Of the approximately 6,000 North American Finns who immigrated to Karelia, Stalin had more than 1,000 killed. If the immigrants who came directly from Finland are included in the total, the number of victims rises to more than 4,000, or around twenty-five percent of the total Finnish population of Karelia. Since the NKVD operated in secrecy, no one will ever know the exact figures.

The pace of Stalin's purges, which can more accurately be described as mass murders, accelerated in the fall of 1935 when Edvard Gylling was removed from office (he was later executed). With Gylling's departure, the dream of Karelian independence began to fall apart. In 1937 and

1938, the Terror reached its peak. Hundreds of people were taken from their homes in the middle of the night. Some died in the gulags, the infamous Russian prison camps, while others were driven to forested areas outside the city, shot through the head execution-style, and buried in mass graves. To this day, bodies are still being discovered on the outskirts of Karelia's capital, Petrozavodsk.

Ironically, the first men to be arrested were those most loyal to the socialist cause. Americans who had joined the Russian Communist Party or had become Russian citizens rarely escaped being imprisoned or killed. However, Stalin was more hesitant to execute immigrants who hadn't surrendered their foreign passports and citizenship papers, because he feared reprisals from other countries.

By targeting the most skilled and educated citizens, Stalin hoped to eliminate anyone he perceived as a threat to his powers. After initially focusing on foreign immigrants — and the Finns weren't the only ethnic minority that he persecuted — Stalin's killing spree expanded to include his own citizenry. Anyone accused of disloyalty was vulnerable. It made no difference whether the charges were true or not, for the accused were not given the opportunity to defend themselves. The liquidations spread so quickly that economic progress came to a halt. Stalin's indiscriminate murdering of farmers, for example, caused a countrywide famine. In all, at least twenty million perished — some say the figure was two or three times that high — during the Terror.

Just as it is impossible to know the exact number of people who died in Stalin's purges, it is even more difficult to know how many escaped from Karelia. Those who returned to the United States or Canada often refused to speak about their experiences. Some feared for the safety of family members who remained in Karelia; others were convinced that Soviet agents might hunt them down. Many were simply embarrassed and wanted to keep their time in Russia a secret. But the primary focus of all the returnees was to put the horror behind them and rebuild their lives.

Families who later tried to determine the fate of relatives who had been arrested rarely had success. No matter how persistent people were in their inquiries, little information was forthcoming from the Soviet government. Though bureaucrats occasionally issued a death certificate listing a fictitious cause of death, the most common response from authorities was silence.

It wasn't until after the breakup of the Soviet Union in the 1990s that the true facts began to emerge. For the first time, researchers were able to visit Karelian archives and track down what had happened to many of the immigrants who had disappeared.

After more than a half century, the silence has finally been broken. Survivors such as Mayme Sevander, Kaarlo Tuomi, Ruth Niskanen, and Lawrence and Sylvia Hokkanen have published moving first-person accounts about what it was like to live under the hand of Stalin's Terror.

Today, historical researchers and the descendants of Karelian immigrants continue to seek the truth of what happened. Web sites have even begun to post the names of Stalin's known victims on the Internet. On one site, the alphabetical list begins with Toimi Aaltio, a man who was born in 1913, immigrated to Karelia in 1931, and was executed on December 2, 1938. From the A's you can scroll down through hundreds of names, reading dates and places of birth, occupations, and finally, execution dates. The list ends with a man named Pekka Yrjölä. Scanning the names of the dead, it is difficult to comprehend how all these bold dreamers, setting out as they did on a journey to build a better world, could come to such a sudden and tragic end. What lesson does it teach us when people so dedicated to a cause can have their fate determined by a single dark moment when boot steps are heard marching in the deepest quiet of the night?